W9-ART-924

POWER PERFECTED IN WEAKNESS

POWER PERFECTED IN WEAKNESS

THE JOURNAL OF
CHRISTOPHER J. KLICKA

FOREWORD BY
JONI EARECKSON TADA

Shepherd Press
Wapwallopen, Pennsylvania

Power Perfected in Weakness
©2010 by Tracy L. Klicka

ISBN: 978-0-9824387-3-2

Published by Shepherd Press
P.O. Box 24
Wapwallopen, Pennsylvania 18660

All rights reserved. No part of this book may be reproduced or utilized in any form or by any means, electronic or mechanical, or by any information storage and retrieval system—except for brief quotations for the purpose of review, without written permission from the publisher.

Unless otherwise indicated, Scripture taken from the New King James Version. Copyright © 1982 by Thomas Nelson, Inc. Used by permission. All rights reserved.

Italics or bold text within Scripture quotations indicate emphasis added.

Page design and typesetting by Lakeside Design Plus
Cover design by Tobias' Outerwear for Books

First Printing, 2010
Printed in the United States of America

JOS   21   20   19   18   17   16   15   14   13   12   11   10
14   13   12   11   10   9   8   7   6   5   4   3   2   1

To our oldest daughter Bethany
who generously spent many hours editing her dad's book.

I know he would be grinning ear to ear
with pride and love were he able to be here with us.

CONTENTS

Foreword

JONI EARECKSON TADA

It happens to every Christian. One minute you're spiritually skipping along; the next, you're staring into the gaping jaws of suffering. It's worse when those same jaws clamp shut around you. Fear and claustrophobia rob you of joy, and pain can become so searing, you dread facing the day—yet when night finally closes in, you pine for the morning.

When suffering like that hits you broadside—such as happened with Chris Klicka—you find yourself searching for a hold on to sanity. You search for someone, anyone who might empathize. That's when Chris and I became close.

We had met years earlier at a small reception in Washington, D.C. Yes, I was impressed with his large and wonderful family, but I was especially touched when he confessed how God had used my books in his life. That's when I learned about his neuromuscular disease—suddenly I had an appreciation for the cane he was leaning on. Little wonder he found the books I had written on suffering such an encouragement, such a comfort.

As Chris's strange form of multiple sclerosis encroached further into his work and family life, the emails between us grew more frequent. I realized, though, that God had not only placed me in his life for his spiritual benefit, but Chris became a blessing to me. Ironically, it was during this time that I was struggling to free myself from the jaws of chronic pain which had clamped around my lower back and hips (how a quadriplegic like me can feel pain is still a mystery . . . but that's another book).

And so, snippets of Psalms and slices of encouraging Scriptures flew between us. Each verse emailed from God's Word reminded us that God's purposes were perfect and that our Savior, intimately acquainted with grief and suffering, was pleading our case before heaven's throne. Occasionally, Chris and I even prayed together on the phone. We did whatever it took to keep our hearts focused on hope.

Looking back, it's clear that God gave Chris the hope he longed for—his hope is now fully realized in heaven. And mine? I'm still discovering the Lord's fresh hope every day. The Spirit of God puts it this way in Isaiah 45:3, "I will give you the treasures of darkness, riches stored in secret places, so that you may know that I am the Lord, the God of Israel, who calls you by name." I still occasionally may feel the dark shadow of pain overwhelm me, but I found heavenly treasures in such darkness: rock solid, unshakable hope. Oh, what a treasure it is to find the Lord of Hope in the midst of any darkness.

That's why I'm honored to write these opening statements for a book about Chris Klicka. As I told him, pain is a strange, dark companion; but a companion, nonetheless. Pain is an unwelcome visitor, but still a visitor. Pain is a bruising of a blessing, but it is a blessing from the hand of God. Who can tell the work of pain in our lives? I know that it drives me closer to that place of fellowship with Jesus that is near, dear, and sweet. So, we take pain as though we were taking the left hand of God—better that than nothing.

And if, for you, that hand ever feels hard, as it often did for Chris during his last months of life on earth, be encouraged with this special paraphrase of Colossians 1:11 from *The Message*: "We pray that you will have the strength to stick it out over the long haul—not the grim strength of gritting your teeth, but the glory-strength God gives. It is strength that endures the unendurable and spills over into joy, thanking the Father who makes us strong enough to take part in everything bright and beautiful that He has for us."

May the following pages bring you glory-strength from God as you are inspired by the story of my friend, Chris Klicka.

—Joni

Joni and Friends International Disability Center
Agoura Hills, California

INTRODUCTION

A LETTER TO THE READER

Dear Friends,

Where does one start to talk about their best companion and lifelong love's earthly end? I remember thinking when I was young, when my parents' friends were celebrating their silver anniversaries, that twenty-five years of marriage was a long time. How differently I feel now. The gift of twenty-five years with Chris, while long, still seems much too short.

Though Chris had multiple sclerosis for fifteen of our twenty-five years together, though we had tremendous challenges and pain along the way because of MS, though we both had to go through the process of letting go of our oneness at the end, so that he could go on to life with Jesus in heaven and I on to life with Jesus here, I am grateful. I am so very grateful for the gift God gave me in Chris.

What first drew me to him back at Grove City College, where we met, was his passion for Christ. His zeal to make Christ known to others around him was the cornerstone of who Chris Klicka was. His deep desire to apply God's Word to all of life, and to help others do that, was part of his spiritual DNA. In this, I have never met his equal.

When God called Chris to the Home School Legal Defense Association (HSLDA) in 1985, to work for homeschooling freedom in the United States and to help build a national organization committed to that purpose, it wasn't his might, his intelligence or his gift of persuasion (something all of our children seem to have inherited from their dad) that God ultimately used. It was his love for Christ and His Word, combined with a tenacity that sometimes drove me crazy, which was the means to magnify God's glory in his life, and to achieve success as an attorney and defender of freedom. Furthermore, it was his love for those he served at HSLDA, homeschoolers all over America and in many countries around the world, that God used to minister hope and help and the gospel of Christ.

Many of you reading this book have followed Chris's work and ministry for several years, and I know that thousands of families have been helped through his dedication and hard work on behalf of homeschoolers while at HSLDA for over twenty-four years. He was not only tireless in his efforts, he was immovable! (1 Corinthians 15:58). He loved his work. Even more, Chris loved the people he served. It brought him great joy to encourage parents as they trained their children in the Lord Jesus and in the Scriptures. His passion for following Christ was demonstrated both in his deep, personal love for God, as well as in how he loved and led our family spiritually.

When he was diagnosed with MS in 1994, Chris purposed in his heart to give God glory in the midst of his MS, and by the wonderful grace which God supplied him, Chris did just that. Your emails, notes and letters these past six months are beautiful tributes to Chris's love for others and his even deeper love for his great Savior, Jesus.

Chris's hope ultimately rested in the finished work of Christ on the cross for his sins, and he knew that one day, whether God chose to heal him of MS in this life or not, he would see Jesus face to face with a new body, free of MS and ready to worship Christ his Redeemer for all of eternity.

Early this year, when Chris's health started to decline more rapidly, he testified of God's power being demonstrated in his life even as he was growing weaker and weaker physically. In addition to speaking at five homeschool conferences last spring, when he was at his weakest in fifteen years, he also started working on this book about the sufficiency of God's power and grace in his life.

Chris was nearly finished with the book when God called him home. He has obtained the Promise, yet if he were able, I know his desire would be to share the hope Christ gave him not only in life but also in death.

And while Chris wasn't able to finish the last few chapters of his book himself, God placed "scribes" around him in the last three weeks of his life, close friends and family who received Chris's last words and observed his final testimony of God's power being perfected in his weakness (2 Corinthians 12:9–10). These dear friends—Dennis and Cathey Alberson, Beth Raley, Stan and LeAnn John, and Bob Farewell—have graciously and humbly assisted us in writing the final chapters of Chris's book as we all observed God writing the final chapter of Chris's life.

And so, dear friends, it is a great honor for me to invite you to read my dear husband's last book. As you read, it is my prayer that Chris's words in this book would reach your heart at its deepest level of need with the encouragement and hope in Christ that Chris so convincingly possessed yet so freely shared while he lived.

To God be all the glory,
Tracy Klicka

PREFACE

The message in this book is simple: "God Can Sustain You Through Anything!"

I must reflect and testify a moment to God's great mercy, kindness, and the blessings He has given me, especially in still having me here after a fifteen-year battle with the worst type of multiple sclerosis (MS).

It has been God and God alone who has carried me this far. If you look behind me, you only see one set of footprints and they are not mine. God, my loving Father has carried me this far.

Many men and women I have met over these last years with progressive-declining MS like me, are either dead by now, or have quit their careers, been on disability for years, or have short-term memory loss and impairing "brain fog." Nearly all of them do not get out of their wheelchair on their own, and none swim. They all get common sicknesses easily. In fact, I have met many people who are completely ambulatory with the less severe relapsing-remitting MS, yet are on disability and spending much of their time making crafts, tinkering around, and trying to avoid stress.

I will never forget this; four years ago, my neurologist, who has had many MS patients over the last thirty-five years, looked me in the face and said, "With your advanced case of MS, you should be bed-ridden. You are doing 100 percent better than all my other patients." All I could tell him then, and all I can say now is "it is not me." It is only the sustaining love and strength of our Father God, Maker of Heaven and Earth.

It is *only* His Holy Spirit power that has kept me alive, given me the "will power" to fight on against the odds, be supernaturally cheerful in the midst of this non-ending trial, and all the while providing for my family of eight, working full time for HSLDA, traveling, swimming for exercise, and allowing my brain and mouth to work better than ever, my legs to stand and walk some.

He has given me a loyal and faithful wife and seven faithful children who all love me and enable me to function every day to do these things. Without them, I could do none of this. That is no exaggeration.

Without the wonderful, faithful service—and prayers—of all of my ten members of the HSLDA legal staff, I would not be able to fulfill my calling at Home School Legal Defense Association as Senior Counsel.

But in this book the most important message I believe God is saying to all of you is this, "No matter what obstacles or trials you face now or in the future, you *can* overcome them and keep on; it is by *My* sustaining grace and power. *I will never leave you or forsake you*!"

If He has sustained me through all of this, He can do the same for you. God truly loves His adopted children.

God bless you all!

—*Chris Klicka*

ALL THINGS WORK TOGETHER FOR GOOD FOR THOSE WHO LOVE HIM

EVEN BAD THINGS

ALL THINGS WORK TOGETHER FOR THE GOOD OF
THOSE WHO LOVE GOD; THOSE WHO ARE CALLED
ACCORDING TO HIS PURPOSE.

—ROMANS 8:28 HCSB

My favorite verse is Romans 8:28. I hang on tightly to this rock-solid promise of God.

This is a fact that we can depend upon, no matter what. Sometimes, as I am going through life with multiple sclerosis, my bodily functions and abilities slowly dying, my spirit begins to despair. However, I remind myself that God's truth remains. It will not change. I can be confident in the knowledge that this suffering I am experiencing will work together for my good and for anyone who knows me and loves God.

God is graciously helping me live it. Let me share two bad situations God turned around for good.

Crying Out to God in the Airport

In April 2007, I traveled with my son Jesse to Denver, Colorado. I was the keynote speaker for a rally in front of the capitol. The Christian Home Educators of Colorado (CHEC) sponsored the rally and expected about 1,000 people; they asked me to speak on freedom and about the need to be eternally vigilant. This was a particularly important rally because the Colorado legislature had switched entirely into Democratic control and threats to the family loomed large. The news had been reporting the arrival of a huge blizzard due to hit the day of the rally.

By faith, I flew to Denver the day before the rally. However, as I was getting off the plane, I lost my balance and fell backwards onto the chair rail. I was in such pain that I could barely breathe. As the airport personnel and my son helped me back to my feet, I felt sick, and every movement brought pain in my back, hip, and kidney area. As I rode away on my scooter, every bump caused searing pain; my stomach felt sick and all I wanted to do was lie down. They ushered me into a room off the main floor of the airport and I quickly lay down on the floor.

With the airport personnel around, I loudly cried out to the Lord for mercy, saying that I could not go on unless He helped me. In spite of the pain, I felt God's call more than ever that He wanted me to speak at the rally.

After I cried out, I felt an extreme peace and calm come over me, and the pain began to subside. The paramedics arrived, checked me out, and urged me to go to the hospital. I told them that I wanted to try to stand and that I had to speak the next day. As I got to my feet once more with their assistance, the pain was 75 percent gone. I decided not to go to the hospital and they made me sign a statement of non-liability. As I did this, I pointed them to Christ. The paramedics left and I had an opportunity to share Christ with the manager of United Airlines who was assisting me. I was able to get on my scooter and that night went out to eat with my son and a good Christian brother.

The day of the rally arrived, but incredibly the blizzard did not. My wife called me that morning and said that the weather pattern had shifted dramatically and the storm had missed Denver. All we could do was praise the Lord. The CHEC leadership and I were praying diligently that the storm would not come, and it didn't. It was unexplainable; basically it was a miracle.

I was able to go to the rally, and in the freezing temperature I felt warm even without a winter coat. The crowd was larger than expected. In fact, over 1,500 people came! Four men carried me up the capitol steps on my scooter, and I was able to address the crowd.

It was a tremendous success and the message of freedom was heard by the legislature loudly and clearly. When I returned home I learned that my hip was out of its socket, but my chiropractor was able to get it back in. Despite the pain, I was able to resume a rigorous swimming routine and returned to my normal MS self.

You can look at this situation in two ways. One way is to just see the horrible pain and difficulty involved in the trip. The other way, God's way, is to see how God answered my cries to Him, brought me healing, and gave me the strength and sufficient grace to complete the mission in Denver. All things work together for good for those who love God and who are called according to His purpose.

The reason we can be so sure of this is to look at the verse following it in Romans 8:

For those He foreknew, He also predestinated to be conformed to the image of His Son, so that He would be the firstborn among many brothers. And those He predestined,

He also called, and those He called, He also justified, and those He justified, He also glorified.

—Romans 8:29–30 HCSB

In other words, God is in control. He is sovereign. That is why all things work together for good. This will never change. We are in the best of hands, no matter what our feelings tell us.

Rushed to the Emergency Room

God gave me a second opportunity to share about Him during a health emergency while in Wisconsin after an extremely successful time of ministry. After I arrived in Wisconsin I talked on a national radio program, spoke four times at the CHEA conference, preached at my parents' church on Sunday morning, and met with my relatives to share God's good news.

I stayed an extra day in Wisconsin at my parents' house and met with some old friends. I was looking forward to the fellowship, and had a Chinese dinner right before they came. They assured us that there was no monosodium glutamate (MSG) in the food and I ate a hearty meal. However, I did not feel well afterwards. Looking back, I think they made a mistake at the restaurant and there actually was MSG in the meal. Since I haven't eaten MSG for years, my body reacted negatively to the small amount in the food.

As my friends began to arrive, my neck and shoulders became stiff at such an extreme rate that I could not continue in conversation with anyone. My arms began to slowly close in around me. I could not stop my arms from gripping me; my hands began to curl up, and my body began to spasm. After about three hours of fighting it and hoping it would pass, I couldn't stand it any longer. My friends had been praying for me and the ones who remained lifted me out of my scooter and laid me on my bed. They tried to pull my arms apart but couldn't. Finally, they called 911 and the ambulance took me to the hospital. I asked my daughter Megan, who accompanied me, to bring tracts and hand them to those in the ambulance. On the way to the hospital I shared Christ with them.

The first person to greet me at the hospital was a born-again Christian nurse and we were able to praise the Lord together. As they gave me an IV with Benadril and muscle relaxant, the symptoms began to go away and I recovered from my allergic reaction to MSG. I shared God's good news with others there also.

As I returned home, the event had quite an impact on all my friends as they saw not only what had happened to me, but they also saw God's faithfulness. The next morning I felt better than I had in months and was able to get into the airplane and fly home. Once again, the Lord showed me that all things work together for good—even these difficult events which ultimately affected my children, my parents, and my friends in a deep and wonderful way by letting them see God's faithfulness.

Romans 8:31–32 says, "What then are we to say about these things? If God is for us, who be against us? He did not even spare His own Son, but offered Him up for us all, how will He not also then with Him grant us everything?" We are the Lord's and He will not forsake us. We have the assurance that God will be with us through whatever difficulty we are facing.

All things work together for good for those who love God. Romans 8 says,

> Who can bring accusation against God's elect? God is the One who justifies. Who is the One who condemns? Christ Jesus is the one who died, but even more, has been raised. He is also at the right hand of God and intercedes for us. Who can separate us from the love of Christ? Can affliction or anguish or persecution or famine or nakedness or danger or sword? As it is written: Because of You we are being put to death all the day long; we are counted as sheep to be slaughtered. No,

in all these things we are more than [conquerors] through
Him who loved us.

—Romans 8:33–37 HCSB

I am more than a conqueror; I am loved. So are you. The
Holy Spirit lives within us and enables us to fulfill the mission
for this world. Nothing can stop us. Nothing can separate us
from the love of God. As it says in Romans 8:38–39, "For
I am persuaded that neither death nor life, nor angels nor
rulers, nor things present, nor things to come, nor powers,
nor height, nor depth, nor any other created thing will have
the power to separate us from the love of God that is in
Christ Jesus our Lord!"

God is on the throne. Whatever you are going through is
not bigger than your Father, God. He will be there to use the
event for His glory, and to work it together for your good.
Praise the Lord!

MY GRACE
IS SUFFICIENT FOR YOU

NOT A TRICKLE BUT AN ENDLESS SUPPLY!

AND HE SAID TO ME, "MY GRACE IS SUFFICIENT
FOR YOU, FOR MY STRENGTH IS MADE PERFECT
IN WEAKNESS." THEREFORE MOST GLADLY I WILL
RATHER BOAST IN MY INFIRMITIES, THAT THE
POWER OF CHRIST MAY REST UPON ME.

—2 CORINTHIANS 12:9

By God's grace, I am sustained by His hand everyday. Despite the increasing decline of my bodily functions, I am trying to be a faithful soldier of the Lord, and I continue to have a strong calling and a clear mission from Him.

So I constantly improvise, adapt, and overcome by the Holy Spirit's power.

All I can do is hang on to God's truth which is unchanging and immoveable. Even though this disease looks unbeatable, I know, that through Christ, I can do all things because He strengthens me (Philippians 4:13). I am assured that greater is He who is in me than he that is in the world (1 John 4:4). I am confident that all things work together for good for those who love God and are called according to His purpose (Romans 8:28), even MS and all the pain and mishaps I experience. I know, absolutely, that power is perfected in weakness so I would rather boast about my weakness that Christ may be seen dwelling in me (2 Corinthians 12:9). Most of all, I know that He has promised an endless supply of His all-sufficient grace.

I have learned to improvise every year in order to complete my God-given mission. I keep re-adjusting how I walk, sit, stand, type, and many other basic functions. I am learning to write and even sign my name with my left hand.

Using the scooter has greatly expanded my horizons. I taught my children how to garden this year while sitting on the scooter; I go on scooter rides almost everyday with my kids, and I go to battlefields, museums, stores, and restaurants using the scooter. It is humbling, but I praise God for "the goodness of the LORD in the land of the living" (Psalm 27:13).

Yet in other ways, God has healed me. I regained my full eyesight and ability to read clearly. God has taken away all depression and has kept my mind very sharp. This is unique when you see the statistics that 70 percent of people with MS experience brain shrinkage, lose their short-term memory, and have "brain fog." My left hand started to get weaker; I cried out to God with all my heart and He brought it back fully. My swimming has become better as I swim twenty-five to thirty laps a day, five to six times a week in my "Endless Pool" (an exercise pool that moves water to create a current). I am keeping my muscles strong with swimming even though many of them I can't use well on land.

Most amazingly, God sustained me through four weekend trips in a row, speaking four to five times each week. It culminated in preaching a sermon in my church the fifth weekend. I never did so much speaking even when I was healthy.

Here is the rest of the story, the miracles of God's power along the way, and His sufficient grace. For a few weeks before my trips I was a little fearful, wondering if I would be able to walk on to a plane anymore? Would I be able to get to bathrooms? Would I be able to stand for a whole hour for my speeches?

The Torn Ligament

I was praying beforehand for my four speaking trips and swimming everyday to be in maximum shape. One day I was walking out of the pool room, and not realizing that the ramp was wet, I slipped on the tile and fell backwards, tearing the ligament in my right knee and falling on the pool control panel. All I could think of was, "How can I do these trips after this fall?"

Every step was painful, and crawling into my bedroom at night was excruciating. The doctor said the torn ligament in my knee would take six weeks to heal and I shouldn't walk at all.

How would I make it?

Then one of my wife's friends invited me to a healing seminar at their church. I listened to the evangelist preach from the Word about Jesus' power to heal. I felt convicted of my sin and began weeping. I went forward in my scooter to have the evangelist pray for me. A lady in the congregation said she saw fire on my legs and another said she saw a cloud, showing God's power in me. As the preacher prayed for the healing of my torn ligament and my MS, he laid hands on me. I was afraid to stand because of the severe pain and told my wife so. Tracy responded, "A twelve-year-old girl just came up to me and said 'The Lord told me to tell you to stand.' "

I stood, with no pain! My knee was healed, and even though it was late at night I walked out of the church without any soreness, after not being able to walk for a week. God graciously healed my knee so that I could go on those four trips to minister to about 10,000 people—in His name.

I still have MS, but His grace is sufficient.

The Power of His Word

As I spoke at each conference, God gave me the words to say, *and* enabled me to stand the whole time for each session. Also, I was able to get on and off the planes. I traveled with one of my children to each state, which normally I didn't do even when I was healthier. God has used that extra time together to bond our hearts closer and gave me a wonderful time to train them much deeper in God's truths. God knows what is best for me *and* my children.

Last year I dragged my laptop and fancy PowerPoint with me to every conference, but the technology would always fail. So God would instead give me the words to say—His words. This year I left my PowerPoint behind and God blessed me mightily again. On the last trip, I tried to use my PowerPoint and guess what? It was mostly blank. So I stopped and prayed for the words and He gave me a new speech. Afterward scores of people came up to me and told me how God changed them and some of them even gave their lives to Christ.

Praise God for His endless supply of grace.

In Everything Give Thanks

Even in Hard Times

Rejoice always, pray without ceasing,
in everything give thanks; for this is the
will of God in Christ Jesus for you.
—1 Thessalonians 5:16–18

Once a year America celebrates Thanksgiving Day. As a family we traditionally write notes about things we're thankful for, and slip them into a homemade mailbox. We read each one aloud at the Thanksgiving dinner table. It is a beautiful, warm time of meditating on God's bountiful blessings. We usually thank God for our family, friends, house, food, freedom, and God's great love for us. It is so important that we recognize God's incredible goodness to us. In fact we all know we should, and many of us do, give thanks to God all year long.

Are We Thankful for the Not-So-Good Things?

But what about the economic recession? What about the change in the political climate and the loss of freedom we are now facing? What about sickness, troubles with our teens or other relationships, the loss of our job, friends that have moved, and other not-so-good things?

We all need to analyze our hearts so that we do not limit our thanks to the good things or only give thanks at certain times. Instead, we need to develop the habit of giving thanks all the time and faithfully thanking God for the not-so-good things.

God makes that very clear in 1 Thessalonians 5:18 when He says, "In *everything* give thanks, for this is the will of God in Christ Jesus for you." Does this really mean we should thank God for everything? Must I even thank God for my gradually deteriorating health due to multiple sclerosis? Do I have to thank Him in spite of losing the use of my legs little by little, and even my right hand?

Yes, I must, because this is God's will for me at this time. I must keep my eyes fixed on Jesus (Hebrews 12:2) and look with spiritual eyes on how *He* is working through these negative circumstances. I must be thankful and show Him and the world that my faith is *real*. I must really believe in His promise in Romans 8:28 that *"all things* work together for good for those who are called according to His purpose."

Although my flesh is hurting so much, I cannot deny that I have seen God work through my MS to change many people's lives. He has, simultaneously, been doing a continuous and awesome work in my heart to conform me to the image of His Son—one day this work on my soul, in all its splendor, will be revealed in heaven. Nor has my MS been in vain for my children, as they learn that the Christian life isn't always a smooth road, but that Jesus will still sustain them. They are learning to be true servants in this process.

God is blessing me with power that is "perfected in weakness" (2 Corinthians 12:9). In fact, Paul says that he would rather boast about his weakness so that Christ may be seen *in him* (2 Corinthians 12:10). I have seen God's promises come true in my life as I find, each day, that His "grace *is* sufficient" for me. He is enabling and will continue to enable me through His Holy Spirit's power to fulfill His calling for me, to be a father to my children, a husband, a homeschool lawyer, an author and a speaker. It is not my power that will enable me to carry on; it is all His!

Therefore, through the tears, I can say, I am thankful for MS—thankful to be counted worthy.

Remember when the disciples joyfully celebrated being persecuted like their Master Jesus had been persecuted? They were thankful to be counted worthy. The same goes for us. We are to give thanks for everything, even the not-so-good things.

Praise and Thanksgiving to God Even in the Midnight Hour

I heard Pastor Tony Evans on the radio one day, explaining that there are three types of thanksgiving or praises: the "cum laude" praises, the "magna cum laude," and the "summa cum laude." He said the "cum laude" praise is when we thank God for our clothes, our marriage, our children, our job; basically, for the good things in life. Certainly it is important that we live thankful lives. I know that if we have a thankful heart every day we are going to have a better attitude despite the circumstances, and be an overcomer of any obstacle in our way. And Jesus will shine brighter through us.

Then Tony Evans said the "magna cum laude" praise is when we are delivered from some bad situation, much like when the ten lepers were healed by Jesus. The one leper came back and was blessed because he thanked God for delivering him from leprosy. How often do we expect the healing when we take the medicine, or expect our next paycheck to take care of the problem and yet don't lean on Jesus and thank Him for His deliverance in those types of situations?

31

Finally, Tony Evans said there is the "summa cum laude" praise. This is when we thank God, even when He hasn't delivered us from our present suffering or trouble. Pastor Evans believes that this type of praise is the most blessed of all. God loves to hear us give Him praise and thanksgiving even in the midst of suffering. When Paul and Silas were in prison, chained, tortured, beaten, and facing a death sentence, the Bible says that they gave praise to God in the "midnight hour" (Acts 16:16–34). It must have been some testimony to the other prisoners and the guards in the prison, to hear them praising and thanking God. Did they feel like doing it? Not on your life. Yet they did it because God deserved the thanks and the praise.

The Bible says that we are to glory in our tribulation and count it all joy when we experience diverse suffering (Romans 5:3–5 and James 1:2–4). Are we being thankful in our "midnight hour?"

Each day, let us be truly and wholly thankful, because we are saved by the blood of Jesus, the Son, and we are going to heaven, and nothing can change that. Scripture says that *nothing* can separate us from the love of God (Romans 8:38–39). Let us be thankful because *all things* work together for good to those who love God, to those who are called according to His purpose (Romans 8:28).

If We Have Jesus, We Have Everything

When visiting Ghana to bring wheelchairs to handicapped people there, Joni Eareckson Tada tells the story (in her book, *When God Weeps*) of a polio victim she met who crawled around on her hands, dragging her useless legs. Joni was amazed that this lady always had a smile on her face. Joni asked her how she could be so happy when she had nothing, her health was so bad, and she didn't even have a wheelchair. The woman had a puzzled look on her face as if she wondered why Joni would ask a question like that. In spite of being a poor beggar, a polio victim, and handicapped in a third-world country, the lady's face shone with joy as she responded emphatically, "*I have Jesus*!"

I do not yet have the faith of that poor girl in Ghana, but I am trusting that God will complete the good work He has begun in me.

If homeschooling is rough this year, if your finances are tight, if your health is shaky, or your friends are forsaking you, you still need to be thankful. God is using each and every circumstance to bring us closer to Him, and make us more like Jesus. That is what we ultimately want, and we have much to be thankful for. Most of all, we can be thankful that we have a God who gives himself to us: His comfort, His never-ending love, His sustaining strength, wisdom, guidance, and overcoming power. He is there with us and will never leave us nor forsake us. Amen!

We Battle Not Against Flesh and Blood

Did You Put Your Armor On?

FINALLY, BE STRONG IN THE LORD AND IN HIS
MIGHTY POWER. PUT ON THE FULL ARMOR
OF GOD SO THAT YOU CAN TAKE YOUR STAND
AGAINST THE DEVIL'S SCHEMES.

—EPHESIANS 6:10–11 NIV

Do you ever feel overwhelmed? Do you ever have a sense
that the world is collapsing on you? Do you sometimes think
that it is better just to give up and quit because life is too
hard, and the road ahead is too difficult?

We all have times in our lives when we feel this way. We feel
we don't have the strength to go on. Everything seems dark
and we feel trapped. Certain circumstances usually dictate
this feeling, such as financial troubles, the death of a loved
one, a bad decision, sickness or disease, a difficult marriage,

friends that turn on us, troubles at work, or ungodly rulers. Often we try to overcome our problems in our own power. We struggle, fret, and complain. Ultimately, we can feel completely helpless and hopeless. We are defeated.

However, this is not God's way. He wants us to put on spiritual eyes and walk by faith. We need to realize that Satan wants to shut us down and shut us up. Satan does not want us to be a witness to others about our Savior, Jesus Christ. He does not want us to be godly fathers and mothers and disciples for Jesus Christ. Satan wants us to be whiners, complainers, quitters, and angry people. He wants our marriages to break up, he wants us to become estranged from our children, to run from our difficulties, and shrink from doing hard things.

But we have to remember to put on the eyes of faith to see that "we do not wrestle against flesh and blood, but against principalities, against powers, against the rulers of the darkness of this age, against spiritual hosts of wickedness in the heavenly places" (Ephesians 6:12). We need to realize that we have to put our armor on and battle the devil, who tries to thwart us from the way that we should go because, as verse 11 says, "put on the whole armor of God *so that you can take your stand* against the devil's schemes."

Yelling in the Night

God has helped me become a spiritual warrior. Never before have I been so aware of the spiritual battle around me, and for two reasons. First, as I struggle more and more with multiple sclerosis and feel a greater weakness and helplessness, Satan tries to take advantage of me. Secondly, as I have victory over the disease and continue to share the gospel one-on-one, and write and speak God's truth before thousands of people each year, Satan's attacks intensify.

For example, in some of my weakest moments, when I can't move a single body part, I start to yell loudly for a few minutes. That is all I can do. I just sit there and scream repeatedly, "I can't take it anymore!" I ask desperately to go home to heaven. I feel like I'm going crazy. Either the pain is too great, or the helplessness and hopelessness is overwhelming.

The other day I felt so terrible and I just wanted to give in and quit. My mind was so dark. It was as if a cloud hung over me. Usually, when these episodes of despair hit me, it takes a few minutes, but God finally reminds me to do spiritual battle. At that point, I cry out to God, quoting scripture, and say, "In Jesus' name, I resist the devil and he must flee from me!" Within minutes, as I declare His Word, the darkness leaves me. Every time, I feel as if a burden has been lifted from my shoulders, a "peace that passes understanding" (Philippians 4:7) flows over me. Once again my mind focuses on Jesus Christ, and once again His grace is sufficient and a way of escape is provided so that I can continue to fulfill His calling. James 4:7 states, "Therefore submit to God. Resist the devil and he will flee from you."

In 1 Peter 5:9, Peter tells us, "Resist him, steadfast in the faith, knowing that the same sufferings are experienced by your brotherhood in the world." Often in these moments of despair, I begin to wrestle in the spiritual world against the devil. I kick him, punch him, and order him to leave. And he does, every time. And I know that sometimes it isn't the devil personally, but one of his demons. Nonetheless, the battle against evil is real and intense.

Trip to the Ohio Homeschool Conference—Almost Thwarted by Satan

I was excited to speak at the Christian Home Educators of Ohio conference. I had decided that it was close enough to drive since, according to MapQuest, it was only six hours to Columbus from my home in Virginia. I chose Bethany, my oldest, and Susanna, my middle child, to accompany and assist me. I figured this would be the last opportunity to take a trip with Bethany before her wedding later that year.

As we set out, we prayed for God's blessing and protection, asking for His angels to surround us. I was well aware of Satan's possible attempt to stop us from doing the Lord's work. I had my Ephesians 6 "full armor" on. As I spiritually put on "the helmet of salvation," I knew I was going to heaven and nothing would change that fact. I was wearing the "breast plate of righteousness" and had my "loins girded with truth" so that I wouldn't listen to Satan's lies and would stand on the promises of God. My "feet were shod with the preparation of the gospel" as I was ready with tracts to witness to those that we met along the way.

Car Trouble

After four hours, we stopped at a gas station. Bethany and I switched places so I could continue the drive. When I turned the key, the car would not start. I figured it must have been the battery. I told Bethany and Susanna to look for the man who earlier had come up to us offering me assistance when my girls were helping me get into the car behind the driver's seat. They found him in a nearby restaurant. He was eager to help. When he heard me turn the key, he said that it wasn't the battery. However, I insisted it was and asked him if he could get some jumper cables. He returned to the restaurant and found someone who pulled their truck next my van and jumped it. The car started right up.

The first gentleman told me where to purchase a battery—there was a store at the next exit. It was around seven o'clock in the evening by this time, and we were concerned that the store would not be open and we would not be able to continue our trip. In the middle of my worries, God gave me perfect peace, and I assured the girls that He would take care of us. Satan just wanted to thwart our trip because he knew I was planning to point people to Jesus in the seven talks that I was scheduled to give at the Ohio conference.

"Be sober, be vigilant, because your adversary the devil walks about like a roaring lion, seeking whom he may devour" (1 Peter 5:8).

We got to the store just in time. Bethany came out with a young man with a battery installation kit who installed a new battery. When I started the car, I yelled out the window "Praise the Lord!" The young man smiled broadly. I thanked him profusely, and Bethany gave him a tract and told him how to be saved.

One Problem After Another

It seemed like our troubles were just starting. As I took an exit to get from one freeway to another freeway, we ran into a traffic jam. It was not for just a few minutes—we were stuck in traffic for over an hour. By that time, we were about three hours behind schedule.

After we got through that mess, more trouble began. The skies opened up a tremendous downpour of rain. It was so bad that I could only see about twenty feet ahead of me on the freeway. Cars were pulling off the road ahead of us. I kept on driving for about a half hour, keeping my speed extremely slow in the pouring rain. Finally, I cried out in exasperation, "Lord, stop this rain!" It was as if He turned off a faucet. The rain stopped, and we were able to continue again at normal speed.

We finally made it to Columbus, and I was careful not to veer off as the freeway split repeatedly. It was almost midnight and we were only two exits away, when suddenly I was in the wrong lane heading off in a different direction on a different freeway. I took the next exit, but did not know how to get back to the original freeway. I pulled over on the shoulder and the girls attempted to figure out where we were on the map. Within minutes, a police officer with his lights blinking pulled over next to us. I told Susanna to roll down the window and the police officer said, "Can I help you?"

I told him we were lost, and he asked me for the address of the hotel, which he plugged into his GPS. We followed his directions and made it safely to our hotel by about 12:30 a.m. I figured that God had sent us an "angel" to guide us to our destination.

We ran into a clerk at the hotel who knew the Lord and took me aside and prayed for my healing after I inquired if he was a Christian. When we got back to the room, I looked at the program for the conference and noticed that I did not speak until 10:30 a.m. I announced that fact to the girls and we were all happy that we could sleep in after such a long and difficult journey. We prayed together, thanking God for His mercies.

And Then I Overslept

The next morning we woke up late to a cell-phone call from my wife, who said water was pouring from the ceiling of our master bedroom. I talked to her for awhile, and tried to counsel her on a course of action regarding the air conditioning unit on the top floor that was overflowing. Meanwhile another phone call came in on the hotel phone. Susanna answered and told them we would be there at the conference at 10:30 a.m. I hung up with my wife and asked Susanna about the call, and she said that the person had indicated that I was supposed to be there at 9:00 a.m. It was already ten minutes until 9:00!

I quickly called the host of the conference and learned that my keynote address was at 9:00 a.m and that there were about 2,000 people waiting for me. She sounded sad but was trying to be positive. I asked her how far away we were from the conference and she replied, "about ten minutes." I asked her how long they could delay and she said until about 9:15. I told her I would be there . . . somehow.

I then explained the situation to the girls and cried out to God asking for His mercy and strength, "For though we walk in the flesh, we do not war according to the flesh. For the weapons of our warfare are not carnal but mighty in God for pulling down strongholds" (2 Corinthians 10:3–4).

My girls got me dressed in record time and into the car, which I quickly drove to the convention center where the convention host was nervously waiting for me. I got into my scooter and followed them into the building through the back way and up the huge freight elevator to the back of the stage. I drove up behind the podium and stood up. The impromptu time of worship and singing by my good friend and a volunteer piano player quickly ended. Incredibly, God gave me the strength to stand during the next hour and deliver His words in a powerful way.

All I can think is that the devil tried to shut me up, but God would not let him. In His name, I went on to speak six more times that weekend. Many people came up to me and told me how my talk touched them and how the Spirit convicted them. They also testified how wonderful the unplanned time of worship was—they were glad I was late.

These stories illustrate how Satan will try, in many ways, to defeat and silence us. We need to be aware and not take that threat lightly. We *must do battle every day*, always crying out to God for grace, strength, wisdom, and protection.

We must hold on to this promise, "The God of peace will soon crush Satan under your feet" (Romans 16:20). We can't lose with God. Even if you are afflicted with a horrible disease like MS, God is bigger, and He will enable you to fulfill His calling for your life.

Go boldly forth, brothers and sisters, each day, no matter what obstacle you face and always remember, "He has delivered us from the power of darkness and conveyed *us* into the kingdom of the Son of His love" (Colossians 1:13).

GOD'S WORD DOES NOT RETURN VOID

WE ARE ON A MISSION FOR THE KING OF KINGS

SO SHALL MY WORD BE THAT GOES FORTH FROM MY
MOUTH; IT SHALL NOT RETURN TO ME VOID, BUT IT
SHALL ACCOMPLISH WHAT I PLEASE, AND IT SHALL
PROSPER IN THE THING FOR WHICH I SENT IT.

—ISAIAH 55:11

Do you know one of the greatest privileges we have here on this earth, that we won't have in heaven? It is the privilege of winning souls for Christ. In heaven, everyone will be saved. There will be an eternity to worship God and praise the Three-in-One. But sharing the gospel with the unsaved won't happen—there will be no more opportunities.

Therefore, let us all purpose in our hearts to reach out to those around us who are stumbling toward hell. Isn't it hard to realize that some of our friends, relatives, and acquaintances are heading to a place of eternal suffering? Proverbs says, "He who wins souls is wise" (Proverbs 11:30). Jesus said, "Follow Me, *and* I will make you fishers of men" (Mathew 4:19). In Isaiah we read, "How beautiful upon the mountains are the feet of him who brings good news . . . who brings glad tidings of good things" (Isaiah 52:7).

We have been saved and can look forward to a place where there will be no more tears, sorrow, pain, death, or sin. As Jesus said, "In My Father's house are many mansions; if it were not so, I would have told you. I go to prepare a place for you" (John 14:2). The reason we are saved is because someone invested time in our lives to share the gospel. Can we do any less for those around us?

Let us share the gospel to those within our reach.

The Bug Man

Our house was invaded by carpenter ants. We called the bug man and Dustin arrived at our house to combat the unwanted insects. When he came to my office to tell me the verdict concerning the problem and the price, I asked him if he knew where he was going when he died. After twenty minutes of discussing the gospel with him, I gave him a Gideon New Testament and "The Charity and Amy Story," which I had written telling about God's miraculous preservation of our twins. If it hadn't been for the ants, I would probably never have met Dustin, but God used a bug invasion to bring this young man within my reach.

Road Trip to Ohio

As already mentioned, I had the opportunity to drive to Ohio with my daughters, Bethany and Susanna, to speak at the state-wide homeschool convention. We were in a convention center, and to reach the stage I had to use a freight elevator. I spoke seven times over the course of the convention, and as I shared many Scriptures and the gospel messages, one person was there every single time: the sound man. That was his job—he didn't have a choice. Finally, after my last talk, God pricked my heart and I drove my scooter over to him and for a few minutes shared the hope that was in me. I gave him a tract that told him how to get to heaven.

Each time we stopped on our drive between Virginia and Ohio, we passed out tracts. At the rest areas my daughters set tracts in different locations, including the trays near the vending machines. As we were loading up again into the car, we saw a little boy walk out holding a tract and then showing it to his mother. She took it and put it in her purse. You never know where the Word of God will go and when it will be read. But you know that if it is read, it will not return void (Isaiah 55:11). God promises that His Word will accomplish His purpose.

After we were about thirty miles from home, we drove through Leesburg, Virginia, and as we passed a semi-truck in a parking lot, my daughter noticed a grandfather clock for sale. I quickly told my daughter to pull over since it was only a few more weeks until our twenty-fifth anniversary, and my wife always wanted a grandfather clock. I stayed in the car and told my daughters to go look at the clock. The man, Wayne, selling this clock by the side of the road, was from North Carolina and had already sold about fifteen grandfather clocks. This was his last one. He gave us a deal that I couldn't refuse and I surprised my wife with this special gift.

I decided to ask Wayne if he was a Christian. When he said no, I began to share with him many Scriptures that told him how to get to heaven. He was divorced, and did not go to church. When I asked him if he was going to heaven, he said, "I hope so." When I asked him what he would say when he was standing at the gates of heaven as to why God should let him in, he said, "I guess because I've been pretty good." I told him that was not good enough, because our works are like "filthy rags" to God (Isaiah 64:6). I told him that being a Christian was about having a relationship with the Son of God. As I told him how he could have this relationship with God, I gave him a Gideon Bible and tract. We arrived home, knowing that we had shared with those within our reach and praying that God would move in the hearts of those with whom we came in contact.

The Water Softener Installers

My wife and I visited our county fair with the children. My wife ended up stopping at a booth that sold water softeners. We have never had one and were interested in the possibility, so she signed up to have a man come to our house to do a demonstration and we ended up purchasing one. Johnny and Matt came to our house to install the water softener and I drove my scooter down the driveway to their truck to ask some questions about the water softener operation. Then I began to ask them each in turn about their eternal salvation. I gave them each a Gideon New Testament and our "Charity and Amy Story" tract. Matt listened and interacted with me and said he would read the materials. Surprisingly, Johnny was really interested. He didn't look like the type—he was kind of gruff. It turns out he had been thinking he needed to go to church because of his young children. He did not know how to get to heaven, but he wanted to know more. This was a perfect opportunity for me to show him the way to heaven. He was visibly elated and exclaimed that he "couldn't wait to come back."

When he came back a couple weeks later to check on the performance of the water softener, I asked him if he had thought more about being a Christian. He said he wanted to "live as a Christian." I rejoiced, and said I would pray for him. I got his email address and sent him information about a local church in his area.

Yes, it is a wonderful blessing to share the gospel story of what Jesus did for us. Share it now to all those within your reach—you will never be sorry.

As Jesus said, "The harvest is plentiful but the workers are few" (Matthew 9:37 NIV).

Go and be "fishers of men!"

ANGELS WATCH OVER US

WE ARE NEVER ALONE

FOR HE WILL COMMAND HIS ANGELS CONCERNING
YOU TO GUARD YOU IN ALL YOUR WAYS; THEY WILL
LIFT YOU UP IN THEIR HANDS, SO THAT YOU WILL
NOT STRIKE YOUR FOOT AGAINST A STONE.
—PSALM 91:11–12 NIV

Do you believe in angels? I certainly do. I have experienced angels at work many times in my life as they have cushioned the blow when I've fallen over 400 times on concrete, marble, bricks, asphalt, wood, and ground of every kind—without ever breaking a bone.

Angels are watching over us. Everywhere we go and whatever we do, we have God's angels protecting us. Hebrews 1:14 states, "Are they not all ministering spirits sent forth to minister for those who will inherit salvation?"

The Scriptures are replete with accounts of the angels making appearances to God's people. For example, two angels came to Lot to rescue him and his family from God's judgment of Sodom and Gomorrah (Genesis 19:15). An angel came to Gideon to prepare him for battle (Judges 6:11–24). An angel was in the lion's den with Daniel (Daniel 6:22) and in the fiery furnace with Shadrach, Meshach, and Abednego (Daniel 3:25). Angels are spoken of in the Old Testament as having great wisdom "knowing all things in the earth" (2 Samuel 14:20). We are told they have great strength (Psalm 103:20) and are very fast (Daniel 9:21).

From Hebrews 12:22, we know that there are "an innumerable company of angels" and that they serve each of us as our guardian angels (Psalm 34:7 and 91:11). As Christians, who are "heirs of salvation," they minister to us (Hebrews 1:14).

In the New Testament, they make many appearances as well. The angel Gabriel came to both Mary and Joseph (Luke 1:26–38 and Matthew 1:19–24). An angel appeared to Elizabeth and her husband to announce the birth of John the Baptist (Luke 1:11). Of course there was a multitude of angels that announced the birth of Jesus (Luke 2:8–15). An angel loosed the bonds of Peter and led him out of prison (Acts 12:5–8). Revelation 2:1 indicates that they are present in each church. Angels escort each believer after they die, into the presence of the Lord (Luke 16:22).

One Saturday night, I experienced the angels at work in saving my life in a harrowing car accident.

Hit-and-Run Car Crash

While returning home after dropping my son Jesse off at the church youth Christmas party, I was driving on a two-way highway, about twenty minutes from my home. The speed limit was fifty-five miles per hour; I was in the process of passing a car and was making my way back into my lane when a car appeared out of the darkness, pulling out of a driveway. It hit me squarely on the left front end of my van.

48

The airbags went off. The crash was so loud that my ears kept ringing for three days after the accident.

Miraculously, I was able to maneuver the van back into the right lane and bring it to a stop, in spite of having blown both front tires and sliding at least seventy-five yards. My arms felt unusually strong and sturdy as I fought the wheel to keep the van from flipping.

My vehicle was totaled but I hit none of the other vehicles on the road. I had no broken bones. No blood. I was traveling almost sixty miles per hour when the car hit me. The police officer at the scene said this type of accident usually resulted in mangled drivers and death.

I know it was angels watching over me. It was God's angels steering my van to safety. God sent His "ministering spirits" to help me in my time of need. The whole time, God gave me an incredible "peace that passes all understanding."

The woman who was driving behind me stopped to see if I was okay; she said she saw a car pull out of the driveway and hit me, but nothing more. The police arrived and tried to find the vehicle that hit me but were never able to find it. They asked around the area where the collision occurred, but apparently nobody knew anything about a vehicle coming or going, or else they were lying to protect the hit-and-run driver.

A policeman, who was a friend of mine, happened to be on duty and was called to assist me at the accident scene and write up the report. I asked how someone would hit another vehicle and then just disappear; he replied that probably the driver was drunk or on drugs, or perhaps they had something illegal to hide in their vehicle.

An Impromptu Missionary Trip

This accident ended up being an impromptu missionary trip. While I was stuck in the car, I was able to talk to the firemen about the Lord. I gave God all the glory for protecting me and taking over at the wheel so that I could control the van during and after the crash.

When I was taken to the emergency room, there were two women paramedics and one man in the back of the ambulance with me during the twenty-minute trip to the hospital. I was able to share the gospel of Jesus Christ. I asked them if they knew where they were going when they died. They were not sure. So I told them how I knew I was going to heaven, where there were no more tears or sorrow—where I would get a brand new body, too. I testified how God's angels had protected me in that terrible accident. I spoke of how short life was and how long eternal punishment was. I quoted many Scriptures to them as I lay strapped tightly to a stiff board. I told them that Jesus is the Way, the Truth and the Life.

I Had a Captive Audience!

I was wheeled into the hospital on the stretcher and God gave me even more opportunities as I talked with the nurses and doctors to give Him the glory for sparing me in the ordeal. While I waited for the x-rays to be processed, I continued to praise the Lord and learned that the technician was a believer; we were able to give God the glory together.

After the doctor reviewed the x-rays, she released me. The x-rays showed that I had no broken bones or major injuries. How could that be in light of the severity of the accident, and the high rate of speed? It was God and God alone. There is no question that He had His angels watching over me.

Angels Stop Our Fifteen-Passenger Van

This incident reminds me of another time, about ten years ago, when my wife was driving our fifteen-passenger van. Five of our children were in the van with her and I was driving behind them in my truck with my son Jesse. My wife went around a curve, and suddenly there was a car in front of her slowing down to make a left turn. My wife tried to swerve but hit the car's back right corner. The van went sliding toward a deep ditch but incredibly stopped only a few feet away from the drop-off.

Pulling off the road behind the van, I got out of the truck and walked to the front of the vehicle to check the damage. To my surprise, I saw drag marks, like two sets of footprints, in front of the van just before the deep, three-and-a-half foot ditch. I knew God had sent two angels to literally stand in front of the van and stop it from going over the edge.

If the van had gone over the edge into the ditch, there would have been members of my family injured since fifteen-passenger vans have a high center of gravity and are notorious for rolling.

Yes, God takes care of His children. Many times He uses His angels to intervene on our behalf. In heaven it will be wonderful to find out how many times God's angels have protected us, throughout our lives, from mishaps and injuries that we didn't even know about.

Praise God, the Maker of Heaven and Earth, and our Redeemer!

FOR THOSE WHO ENDURE TRIALS

THERE IS A CROWN OF LIFE AWAITING

BLESSED IS THE MAN WHO ENDURES [TRIAL]; FOR
WHEN HE HAS BEEN APPROVED, HE WILL RECEIVE
THE CROWN OF LIFE WHICH THE LORD HAS
PROMISED TO THOSE WHO LOVE HIM.

—JAMES 1:12

Sometimes hardships and difficulties come upon us and we don't understand why. We know that God is sovereign and in control of all things. We know that all things work together for good for those who love God. We know we can do all things through Christ who strengthens us. But sometimes it still doesn't make a lot of sense. Nonetheless, God tells us, "My brethren, count it all joy when you fall into various trials" (James 1:2).

This sounds like the old adage, "Grin and bear it." Is that all it is? God just wants us to get used to it? I think there is far more to our struggles than that. For instance, here are two difficult situations I found myself in—above the daily struggles of living with this dread disease. In each situation, God brought a trial that ultimately strengthened my faith.

Burning on Hot Asphalt

When I was in the midst of my homeschool conference season one year, my scooter throttle began to malfunction. I decided to bring it into the scooter repair shop.

First, my son Jesse and I stopped at the chiropractor. Even though it was hot outside, I felt good. The adjustment had gone well and the heat hadn't made me as weak as it usually did. On the way to the scooter repair place, I decided to let Jesse practice driving. We got there, dropped off the scooter and were told it would be ready for us within the hour. We decided to stay in town and have some lunch. When we returned, Jesse kept the car running and went inside to get the scooter. I leaned back on the passenger side to sleep and woke up forty-five minutes later in a car that was incredibly hot—so hot that the heat had paralyzed me.

I was finally able to raise my arm enough to start beeping the horn and Jesse came out in a few minutes, but I was completely exhausted. My joints were in great pain, I could barely talk and my head was throbbing. It was so hard to understand what God was doing. I could only sit there and try to not sin with my lips. Even though I felt horrible, I kept saying, "God, you give and you take away. Blessed be the name of the Lord." In times like these all one can do is simply trust Him.

Little did I know the ordeal was not over—not by a long shot.

During the drive home I could barely recover from the intense weakness brought on by the heat. When we got home, Jesse swung my legs out of the van and I stood up.

Unfortunately, my legs gave out and I fell down to the ground in a squat. My knees do not bend completely due to the MS, so the pain was excruciating, almost causing me to black out.

I yelled to Jesse to yank my legs out from under me so he could extend them to relieve the horrible pain. My upper body was wedged into the lower part of the door for a moment, and then I slipped onto the scorching hot, black asphalt in the 100 degree heat outside.

As I lay on the hot black asphalt of our driveway, I cried out to my Lord for mercy and yelled to Jesse to get help. My shirt had come up, so my bare back was burning on the asphalt! Jesse ran inside and returned with my wife and a couple of the children. They lifted me onto the scooter, but I was so weak I couldn't even drive the scooter into the house.

Once inside, my family laid me on the bed and began to put ice packs on me in an attempt to cool me down. I prayed, "Have mercy on me, O Son of David!" Miraculously, within fifteen minutes I was mostly recovered and was able to go to my office and begin to work. Within two days I was flying to Oklahoma City to minister in His name to 2,800 people—all by the power of the Holy Spirit.

Why did all this happen?

Remember the verse I quoted at the beginning of this chapter? "My brethren, count it all joy when you fall into various trials." But what else does James 1 go on to say in verses 3–4, and 12? God tells us why these trials happen, ". . . knowing that the testing of your faith produces patience. But let patience have its perfect work, that you may be perfect and complete, lacking nothing."

> Blessed is the man who endures [trial]; for when he has been approved, he will receive the crown of life which the Lord has promised to those who love Him.
>
> —James 1:12

God is telling us that when we go through these trials and temptations, it is not in vain. It has purpose—it is a test. Is our faith real? Or do we only have joy when everything is going our way and we can easily see God's goodness? Can we walk through these times by faith if not by sight? Do we really believe God's promise in Romans 8:28 that says, "All things work together for good for those who love God and are called according to His purpose?"

Through these hard times, He is producing in us patience, and this supernaturally-created patience *will make us complete*, lacking nothing. Wow! That means that if we love and trust Him and never give up during these various trials we will have everything. God, our loving Daddy, is proving our faith.

A Mini-tornado and a Computer Crash

After a six-day, ministry-packed trip to Wisconsin with three of my children (I did a one-hour live, national radio talk show, spoke three days at the Wisconsin homeschool convention, and preached a sermon at my Mom's church), I came home to 100 degree weather.

As I was swimming and exercising in my pool, I saw the sky suddenly darken. Within moments, a microburst storm came down our street, ripping out the trees in our front yard and pulling siding off the house. The downpour was extraordinary. Then the power went out due to a tree pulling down a power line. Since I couldn't swim anymore because the current in the pool is created by an electrically-run fan, I had Jesse help me out of the pool.

As I sat in the house, it got warmer and warmer and after eight hours of no power and no air-conditioning, I started getting weaker and weaker from the heat. I made a decision to get a reservation in a nearby hotel. I called several of them and they said that they were all filled up with others in the same predicament, but I was finally able to find one with a room.

The five children loaded me up, packed some bags in the van, and we checked into the Hampton Inn down the road—all of us in one room. At least now I could get air conditioning and avoid becoming completely paralyzed. We had a special opportunity to share the gospel with the hotel clerk, and we had a great time of devotions in our room; these were heaven-sent moments.

Then, for me, the battles began again. I tried to sleep, but woke up five times throughout the night, having to go to the bathroom. Each time I had to swing myself off the high bed and onto the ground never knowing how I would land. I repeatedly hurt myself as I twisted my body, and I had to wake Jesse each time to help me get back in bed.

All I could say was, "Not my will, but Thine be done." Perhaps God was just giving me some exercise. The next morning my wife came to the hotel and there we had a previously-scheduled meeting with our pastor. I felt strong and knew this was all from God. His grace was sufficient once again.

When I returned home I found that although the power was back, I had lost my computer's hard drive due to the storm. Even though it was turned off and had a surge protector, a lightning bolt must have landed nearby and gone right through the electric socket, frying my computer. I lost all my personal writings like my poems, articles, personal injury case files, and wills that I had written for other people over the years. It turned out nothing was recoverable—I had no back up.

Why? What purpose? Isn't MS bad enough?

But God spoke to me from His word in 2 Corinthians saying, do not lose heart. Though your outward man is perishing, your inner man is being renewed day by day. This momentary light affliction is *nothing* compared to the glory that awaits you. What you see is temporary, what you do not see is *eternal* (see 2 Corinthians 4:16–18).

I resolved again to love my Savior, never give up, and endure the trials because a crown of life awaits me in glory. Praise God! Even in the midst of our trials, He is helping us to endure and He has promised us a crown of life.

No Good Thing Does God Withhold

From Those Who Love Him

For the LORD God is a sun and shield;
The LORD will give grace and glory;
No good thing will He withhold from
those who walk uprightly.

—Psalm 84:11

Sometimes I feel sorry for myself.

I think, "I have it pretty bad. I have progressive-declining multiple sclerosis; the worst kind. I can't run, participate in anything athletic, roll over in bed, eat what I want, pick things up, carry things, type with my right hand, do buttons, dress and undress myself, and on and on. I am physically dependent."

A couple of weeks ago, I was kneeling next to my bed, whining to God about my situation. And frankly, I was forgetting His promises.

A Still, Small Voice

I prayed to God saying, "You do not need me to stay here. Please take me home. You do not need me at HSLDA helping homeschoolers. You can get someone else. You do not need me for my wife and children anymore. You can get someone else. You just don't need me."

Then, for the first time in my life, I unmistakably heard God speak in "a still, small voice." In my mind, as clearly as someone talking to me, I heard Him say, "But I have chosen you to strengthen believers. I have chosen you to be a witness to the unbeliever. And I won't let you down. I have chosen you to be part of the special fellowship of my suffering."

Immediately, hope welled up in my heart. God restored my will to go on. I was not any stronger physically, but my spirit was renewed. God soon confirmed His message to me. In a few days my son Jesse and I drove from Virginia to Buffalo, New York, to join homeschool leaders from around the country, and the world, at the Alliance and HSLDA homeschool leadership conferences. Over the next few days, even though my body was weak, and I experienced hardship, God was "hugging" me every time I turned around.

I received hugs from many wonderful friends whom I had known for a long time. Over and over again, I was told that my being there, my attitude and my devotional emails, were being used to strengthen the faith of many, and helping them to keep on keeping on. Wow!

> I will praise You, O LORD, with my whole heart; I will tell of all Your marvelous works. I will be glad and rejoice in You; I will sing praise to Your name, O Most High . . . The LORD also will be a refuge for the oppressed, a refuge in times of trouble. And those who know Your name will put

their trust in You; for You, LORD, have not forsaken those who seek you.

—Psalm 9:1–2, 9–10

Once again the Lord showed me that He was real, and that He loved me. Once again, He showed me that it was "necessary for their sakes that I stay" (Philippians 1:24). I just needed to trust *Him*.

God Is the God Who Heals

One day in August 2007, the day before my daughter Bethany was to be married, I was feeling physically weak. In fact, that whole month of August, I felt that I was sliding downhill in terms of my health. And my one strong hand was getting weaker, which always scares me. I sent out an email to my friends and homeschool leaders and asked them for prayer.

I am here to testify that God heard those many prayers lifted to His throne and He had mercy on me. Throughout the day I became stronger and stronger and was able to sleep through the night; in the morning I got out of bed by myself for the first time in weeks. I was dressed and driven over to the church, where my oldest daughter Bethany was to be married.

God graciously gave me strength to stand during the service and to stand for all the pictures with my family. During the reception I felt great. I met many old friends who had come to celebrate the day with us.

God *is* the God of miracles. Always remember that. He is able. He healed in the Old and New Testaments and the Scriptures say that "Jesus Christ is the same yesterday, today and forever" (Hebrews 13:8).

Crying Out to God, and He Delivers

After arriving home from a week-long trip to Buffalo, New York, I ate some Chinese food. It had been about two years since I had eaten Chinese food. The last time I tried Chinese I was in Wisconsin for a homeschool conference, and I had an allergic reaction due to the MSG and ended up going to the hospital. This time I made sure to check with the restaurant and they told us there was no MSG in the food.

After dinner, we celebrated my son Jesse's sixteenth birthday. As we opened the presents, my stomach began to hurt more and more intensely. Finally, I could stand it no more, and I yelled to my family to quickly lay me down on the couch. I continued to groan and yell in extreme pain. My wife wondered if I should go to the hospital. The pain would not subside, and I was at my wit's end. I cried out, "Have mercy on me, O Son of David. Have mercy on me, O Son of David. Have mercy on me, O Son of David!"

Immediately—and I mean immediately, God stopped the pain entirely. And the pain never returned. I called my family back together and told them of God's faithfulness and deliverance. We rejoiced together and then continued to celebrate my son's birthday.

No Good Thing Does God Withhold from His People

God's promises are true.

We are promised, "For the Lord God is a sun and a shield; the Lord will give grace and glory; no good thing will He withhold from those who walk uprightly" (Psalm 84:11).

I am blessed. He always gives His children "the grace sufficient" (2 Corinthians 12:9), and "a way of escape" (1 Corinthians 10:13) so that we can bear whatever it is that we are going through.

What Job learned when he heard from God in the whirlwind (Job 38:1), I too am learning. I have no right to complain. God knows that I am but flesh, but He is a forgiving God who is faithful and just to forgive us our sins if we confess them (1 John 1:9).

Praise God for His great love, compassion, forgiveness, and salvation. The Lord is our sun and shield—truly no good thing does He withhold from us.

Remember, to fully understand this we have to know Romans 8:28, "All things work together for good for those who love God and are called according to His purpose." Even though the pain and suffering may not be considered good at the moment, God will—and that's a promise—He will work all things together for good. We can count on it.

This causes me to reflect on my life, and I realize again that people do not need to feel sorry for me. I am a child of the King. I'm going to heaven one day. No one can snatch me out of the Savior's hand. He has blessed me tremendously in so many ways, in my past and in my present.

I thought I would attach a poem that I wrote a while ago for my children that captures the sentiment that I should always have: a perspective of thankfulness for God's goodness that He has abundantly poured over me.

My Children, Don't Feel Sorry For Me

I long to hike a thousand trails
And have the strength in these feeble knees.
I yearn to run, jump, and climb
But my Father ordained this disease.

I wish I could play basketball with you
And take my sweetheart to a dance.
I would love to carry heavy things again
Or climb on rocks, taking a chance.

Oh, how I miss kicking a ball across the field
And running hard 'round a track.
I wish I could just roll over in bed.
I so want to turn the clock back.

Yet don't feel sorry for me.
Listen to what God's let me do.
God has always been good to me,
With eagle's wings I flew.

Sure my hands and legs are now weak
But for forty years they worked swell.
I even played most every sport
And lifted two hundred and five pounds well.

Please don't feel sorry for me.
I pitched many winning games.
I was a center and running back
And fired guns with a steady aim.

I crawled through dark, dangerous caverns,
Backpacked the Appalachian Trail.
I repelled cliffs backwards and forwards,
All my muscles worked without fail.

My children, do not feel sorry for me!
God has let me do so much.
I was strong once like all of you,
I wrestled and tumbled and such.

For twenty years, I planted and grew gardens,
I painted whole houses 'til done.
I did carpentry, landscaping, and mechanics
And asphalted lots in the burning sun.

Don't ever feel sorry for me!
For I am blessed beyond belief.
God has used me to build His kingdom
When I cried out, He gave relief.

He has given me the very best wife.
A great job and cause that is rare.
Seven wonderful, loving children,
And thousands who lift me up in prayer.

Hey, don't feel sorry for me!
Mom and I have traveled thousands of miles.
Across South Africa, Europe, Japan
Speaking on homeschooling all the while.

We have been on safaris and windjammer ships
Locomotives and planes of all kinds.
I have driven ski dos, snowmobiles, and speed boats
And any scooter, cycle, and bike I'd find.

Really, don't feel sorry for me!
When I fight to walk or fall hard to the ground.
I've already lived a whole life in years
Used by God to help thousands the world around.

I've journeyed to all fifty states
Visiting oceans, mountains, and desert lands.
I've seen wildlife, battlefields, and big cities,
And touched ages of history with my hand.

I have argued before three Supreme Courts
Testified before many legislatures and boards.
Influenced Congress to change laws for good
And witnessed to thousands about our Lord.

Oh yes, don't feel sorry for me!
Because I don't eat fast foods or treats.
In youth, I enjoyed hundreds of donuts,
And tasted most every snack or sweet.

I ate cheese and sausages by the pound
And hot dogs and hamburgers a lot.
I drank milk, sodas, and shakes too
And had much ice cream and many a brat.

Just don't feel sorry for me!
Even though I sometimes complain.
I admit life is so very hard
But God is with me through the pain.

I am saved by the blood of the Lamb.
He has prepared a perfect place for me.
This is truly "momentary light affliction,"
Nothing compared to life in eternity.

Please, please don't feel sorry for me
God has given me countless blessings.
He faithfully carries me through the deep waters
He makes my spirit soar on eagle's wings.

Just don't let this disease be in vain for you
Keep holding on to your Father God tight.
God has ordained my MS lessons for all of you
To teach you to love and obey Him with all your might.

Oh, try not to feel too sorry for your daddy!
Though my bodily functions slowly die
My soul is forever safe; I will be all right
Yet it hurts my heart and I may sometimes cry.

I want more than anything else you can do
To faithfully honor your mom with love.
Help her, obey her, and bless her always.
She is a precious gift from your Father above.

And submit to God and resist the devil—he'll flee.
Draw near to God and He will draw near to you.
Love Him and keep His commandments.
Honor Him and God will honor you.

Endure and you will reign with Him
Deny God and He will deny you.
When we are faithless, He is still faithful
His grace is sufficient to carry you through.

But I will fight the good fight and keep the faith
With a scooter, running the race to win.
Keeping my eyes fixed on Jesus Christ,
Until I am free from this body of sin.

Marantha! Lord quickly come!

I have no greater joy than this, to hear of my children walking in the truth.

—3 John 4 NASB

NEVER GIVE UP BUT PERSEVERE

RUN THE RACE TO WIN

DO YOU NOT KNOW THAT THOSE WHO RUN IN A
RACE ALL RUN, BUT ONE RECEIVES THE PRIZE?
RUN IN SUCH A WAY THAT YOU MAY OBTAIN IT.
—1 CORINTHIANS 9:24

Life does not always go the way we want it to, does it?

We get sick, have accidents, our kids disappoint us, friends move, possessions break or become lost, people unjustly judge us, the economy turns down, our expenses get too high, close relationships sour, loved ones die, we have too much work, the government takes away a little more freedom, our homeschooling does not go the way we planned, we suffer some hardship, and on and on.

These disappointments are unavoidable. In fact, we cannot even think we are the only ones experiencing these difficult times because God tells us, "No temptation has seized you except what is common to man . . ." (1 Corinthians 10:13). We are not alone in our hurt and pain. As one friend told me, "The grass is always browner on the other side of the fence!"

So we understand what Job meant when he said, "God gives *and* takes away" (Job 1:21). Bad things will happen to good people, but that is not the end of the discussion. There is a promise in the rest of that verse in 1 Corinthians, it is from the Maker of heaven and earth, whom we can count on—"But God is faithful, who will not allow you to be tempted beyond what you are able, but with temptation will also make the way of escape, that you may be able to bear it" (1 Corinthians 10:13).

Unlike the world, even in the most difficult times, we cannot lose; we are told, "For whatever is born of God overcomes the world. And this is the victory that has overcome the world—our faith. Who is he who overcomes the world, but he who believes that Jesus is the son of God?" (1 John 5:4–5), and we are taught that, "You are of God, little children, and have overcome them, because He who is in you is greater than he who is in the world" (1 John 4:4).

Let that truth sink in—we will overcome! We cannot lose, no matter how dark the road or how great the pain. And how do we overcome the difficult circumstances we are in? Do we pray and God just removes the problem? He might—and sometimes He does—but it is His choice.

So how do we overcome? It is by faith. We must trust God in the midst of a time of disappointment and suffering even though we do not see Him. We must have faith that God's promise is true that, "All things work together for good for those who love God and are called according to His purpose" (Romans 8:28). We have to persevere and run the race *to win*. As Paul tells us in 1 Corinthians 9:24, we can't just run the race, but rather we have to run in such a way that we receive the prize.

What great assurance this is for me as I travel this difficult existence of debilitating multiple sclerosis which has made me such a dependent—depending on my children in order to live and work! And His Word also declares, "Yet in all these things we are more than conquerors through Him who loved us" (Romans 8:37).

Praise God! We are the victors, not only in eternity, but now!

Wiping Out in Church

In December, I was trying to "make lemonade out of the lemons" and driving full speed on my scooter, going down the hall at our church to the bathroom with my son John standing on the back of the scooter. I was weaving and we were laughing. Then one of John's friends playfully lunged at him and John suddenly leaned all his weight to one side causing the scooter to pitch over onto its side on the granite floor, crushing my shoulder and knocking it painfully out of its socket again.

But the angels kept my head off the floor! As I lay there in pain with the scooter on top of me, God gave me the ability to be "more than a conqueror" and declare, "Blessed be the name of the Lord" to those who rushed to help me. And then God gave me the victory in another battle in His holy war as I said, by faith, "God just gave me a Holy Spirit chiropractic adjustment!" When friends pulled me up off the ground, I could actually stand up better and stronger than before. All things work together for good, and I'm still in the race.

Off the Ramp!

As a surprise Christmas gift for my wife, I bought two plane tickets to Florida and arranged for us to attend some friends' book retreat. On the plane, I was providentially switched to bulk head seats right across from a business executive named Neil. I struck up a conversation and was able to share Christ with him—he received the tract and eagerly accepted my challenge to read the Bible. Our friends blessed us at the retreat as Tracy and I ministered to the attendees. Then, when I was going up a ramp, I hit a bump and my scooter wheel went off the side of the ramp and I hit the ground on my bad shoulder again. This time I fell from an elevated position which would have hurt much worse except God's angels had me fall on the soft Florida soil. Once again, I was able to verbally praise God through the pain and testify about His mercy as my friends picked me up. Although I had physical pain for the rest of the trip, God refreshed Tracy's and my relationship.

On the way home, I sat again in a different seat, away from my wife, next to Ryan. He was a young college student from California and he soaked up the gospel message I gave him. I also looked in my backpack and I found a perfect gift for him—a book on the faith of William Wilberforce, which he welcomed because he had nothing to read on his long flight to California.

God is teaching me to keep persevering, ". . . knowing that the testing of your faith produces patience. But let patience have its perfect work, that you may be perfect and complete, lacking nothing" (James 1:3–4).

Vindictive Fencing of Our Lake

After seventeen years of access to the lake we live on, a harsh and mean-spirited developer has built a fence and put up "no trespassing" signs, blocking us and our neighbors from access to the lake. He did it along with mocking me personally, attacking my reputation, and cursing at me to the other neighbors. I could not believe it. I was being attacked in my own backyard—and right in the middle of intense HSLDA work during the legislative season. I rallied my neighbors, organized meetings, wrote letters to county officials, and met with the millionaire developer explaining our legal right of access based on our implied easement, all to no avail. I started to worry and fret and my arm started to get worse from MS. I had let down "my shield of faith" and Satan's fiery darts were hitting me. I was getting angry. I even went to the hospital and got a prednisone treatment hoping it would help.

Then God answered me as I cried out to Him about my inner helplessness and despair. He reminded me from His Word, "Be anxious for nothing, but in everything by prayer and supplication, with thanksgiving, let your requests be made known to God; and the peace of God, which surpasses all understanding, will guard your hearts and minds through Christ Jesus" (Philippians 4:6–7).

Now with God's supernatural peace I could fix my eyes on Jesus again, instead of my circumstances. The lake trouble was opening a huge door to my unsaved neighbors and county officials. I got everyone's email and have been meeting and calling them all regularly as we battle to save our lake, sharing the gospel in the process and exhibiting the fruits of the Spirit. Permanent relationships with about seven families are being established. Now I am in the process of filing a lawsuit to recognize our right of access, as I continually help build my neighbors' resolve not to give up—no more worries, mate!

God is my defender. He is in control and as long as He's on the throne, I can keep persevering and running the race.

Meanwhile, my attempt to seek relief through prednisone backfired—it made me worse and I went through horrible side effects and terrible nights. Yet God gave me a way of escape as Jesse, my son, slept with me during the worst week, helping me endure. I know God is building Jesse's character and his dependence on God's strength. Throughout the five days of visits to the hospital, John and Amy or Charity and Susanna would come with me and pass out dozens of gospel tracts to patients and visitors. I was able to share the gospel with many people there.

God reminded me, "We are hard pressed on every side, yet not crushed; we are perplexed, but not in despair; persecuted, but not forsaken; struck down but not destroyed" (2 Corinthians 4:8–9). By God's grace *alone*, I can go on ministering, working, living and providing for my family.

God heard my cries and wiped away the bad side effects of prednisone, just in time for me to speak six times in California and five times in New Mexico. Satan tried to neutralize me and stop God's message from going forth, but God turned it around. I was able to give the gospel to 2,500 people at a New Mexico graduation.

On top of it all, God enabled me to stay with good friends in New Mexico and spend an extra five days seeing God's glorious creation with Jesse, Susanna, and Charity. My kids had the time of their life.

God is good all the time!

Remember, no matter what difficulties you go through, persevere by God's strength—*His grace will see you through and enable you to bear it!*

> Therefore do not cast away your confidence, which has great reward. For you have need of endurance, so that after you have done the will of God, you may receive the promise.
> —Hebrews 10:35–36

GOD WILL GIVE US A WAY OF ESCAPE

HE LOVES US SO

NO TEMPTATION HAS OVERTAKEN YOU EXCEPT
SUCH AS IS COMMON TO MAN; BUT GOD IS
FAITHFUL, WHO WILL NOT ALLOW YOU TO BE
TEMPTED BEYOND WHAT YOU ARE ABLE, BUT WITH
THE TEMPTATION WILL ALSO MAKE THE WAY OF
ESCAPE, THAT YOU MAY BE ABLE TO BEAR IT.
—1 CORINTHIANS 10:13

God has shown me many wonderful and fearful things as I confront the long, arduous battle with this disease.

I would never have thought, as a young Christian lawyer with a burning call in my heart to serve God, that He would assign me this mission. He has told me to climb a Hill of Difficulty that only seems to get steeper. Yet as a good soldier, I must continue and complete this mission and take the hill.

He tells me to just trust and obey—that He will equip me and sustain me.

I am to concentrate on keeping my eyes fixed on Jesus while I run the race with endurance (with a scooter), and try to bring Him glory in all that I say and do, even in the pain and suffering. In the midst of each trial I go through, He has always proved faithful and has never given me more than I can bear.

These truths could not have been made more evident by the Lord than a few weeks ago when He delivered me from a near disaster. We had just had a snow storm that delivered fourteen inches of snow. Two days later, I prepared to go to work, using all my strength to shuffle to the sink without my foot braces. I had just gotten a chiropractic adjustment and I looked forward to feeling a little better. Within a minute or two into shaving, as I leaned on the sink for balance, my feet slipped out.

I fell hard on the wood floor, shattering my watchband and knocking my shoulder out of its socket. I calculated that it was about my 400th fall in the last few years—but God has never let my bones be broken.

I yelled. I railed at the Lord. I told Him that He was trying to kill me. I bitterly told Him to just get it over with. He did not need me one bit. I begged Him to take me home. I got dressed and left, grumping loudly, heading toward HSLDA's office with Susanna and Charity.

After driving for about an hour, I suddenly drifted to the right and hit a snow bank going about fifty miles per hour. My car was sucked into a ditch, and then I hit a thirty-foot snow-covered ridge. The car was out of control and I felt it bouncing violently and lurching as it seemed about to flip over—in fact I knew it had to flip because the ridge we were heading toward was slanted nearly straight up.

But God supernaturally intervened. He took over the wheel, and my right arm, partially out of its socket, became like a band of steel. I gained control, drove off the ridge, through the snow bank and back onto the road, going forty-five miles per hour.

Immediately, I prayed and thanked God.

And God said to me—crystal clear in my mind—"See, I could have taken your life just moments ago. But instead I sustained you through the impossible, and the car did not flip. In the same way, although this road of suffering seems impossible, with MS destroying your bodily functions, I will sustain you!" I immediately repented from my earlier bitter attitude and asked God to forgive me. Instantly, I felt a heavy burden lifted off me.

On the way home, we looked for the ridge and every ridge we saw was covered with trees, stumps, huge thickets, and street signs—except for one that was completely bare and open. And it had tire tracks across it in the snow. My kids and I laughed as we thought of what people must have thought as they drove by, wondering "Why in the world was that car driven on that snowy ridge? Was he crazy?"

My life is not my own—it is God's. My limbs are not my own—they are His. I must trust Him. I must say with Job, "Though He slay me, yet will I trust Him!" (Job 13:15). I must say with Jesus, "Not my will but your will be done," and really mean it in my heart.

I am learning to be more like Jesus, but it is painful. The tests keep coming all the time.

A month ago, I thought maybe I was getting better. I got adjusted by the chiropractor and I walked out feeling good. I had four steps left to get to the car and suddenly my cane snapped. I fell on the concrete, messing up my back again. Everyone had gone out to lunch and somehow I managed to grab the bar on the glass door and pull myself up, but it again set my health back.

I was riding down my driveway at night in my scooter to go to a play my daughters were in and as I rounded the bend, I flipped the scooter on the gravel. Boy, did that hurt. I made it to the play but I could not walk at all.

So many obstacles. And they keep coming. Yet God enables me to somehow live, witness to many for Jesus, teach and train my kids, teach AWANA every Friday night, teach a government class to twelve homeschool high schoolers every Monday night, work full-time for HSLDA, exercise two hours a day, and, when I get my windows of strength, do weightlifting, stationary biking, 500 paces, leg exercises of every kind, and swimming about thirty laps against a current, four days a week.

How? Through God and God alone. To Him be all the glory!

I am operating on the Holy Spirit's power. He is the one that enables me to persevere, and He is the one who provides a way of escape. God gives and takes away. My heart chooses to say, "Blessed be your name!"

As A.W. Pink once said in his book *The Sovereignty of God*, "But the man of faith brings in God, looks at everything from his standpoint, estimates values by spiritual standards, and views life in the light of eternity. Doing this, he receives whatever comes as from the hand of God. Doing this, his heart is calm in the midst of the storm. Doing this, he rejoices in hope of the glory of God."

WHEN THE WAVES GET HIGH

KEEP YOUR EYES FIXED ON JESUS

IN THE DAY OF MY TROUBLE I WILL CALL UPON
YOU, FOR YOU WILL ANSWER ME.
—PSALM 86:7

Did you ever have one of those days when everything seems to go wrong? In fact did you ever have one of those weeks? Or maybe one of those months or even years when everything goes wrong?

I have had a debilitating disease for fifteen years, steadily losing control of my body. From the outside, it looks hopeless. When my wife and I were married and took the vows promising we would be true in sickness or in health, we did not imagine what that actually meant. When I was diagnosed with multiple sclerosis in 1994, my life was turned upside down. I didn't want to face what multiple sclerosis would do, but it immediately began debilitating me, quickly forcing me to depend on a cane. However, God had other plans and He resurrected me through a changed diet and lots of prayers by many people, and I was able to put away my cane and live more normally for the next four years. But, God allowed the disease to come back, and now it's at the point where I am a dependent.

Where Is God?

Has God abandoned me? Is God unable to heal me? Of course not! In fact, He gives something greater to me than healing—He gives himself! He gave himself for us all through His Son's death on the cross *and* He gives himself through the constant presence and indwelling Holy Spirit who is our Comforter. He promises us in His Word in Romans 8 that He will never leave us or forsake us. Nothing can separate us from His love.

"For I am persuaded neither death nor life, nor angels nor rulers, nor things present nor things to come, nor powers, nor height, nor depth, nor any other created thing will have the power to separate us from the love of God that is in Christ Jesus our Lord" (Romans 8:38–39 HCSB). That's a promise that we can stand on and trust forever.

When Everything Seems to Go Wrong

In July 2007, with the use of a hyperbaric oxygen chamber, I was making great progress. I was increasing my weight-lifting, my swimming strokes, my walking, and my memory was getting better—everything was improving for the first time in years.

But then things began to go more wrong than ever. As I headed to the chiropractor, a man driving a Mack truck wasn't watching where he was going and ran into the back of my minivan. The truck was owned by a gigantic construction company and they are denying liability, claiming that I somehow hit the truck.

Then our John Deere tractor broke down, and the furnace and air conditioning died. I got extremely weak from the heat plus it cost us $12,000 to replace. Our bathroom water pipe burst upstairs and flooded the ceiling, and it turned out that all the plumbing in our house was faulty and needed to be replaced—to the tune of thousands of dollars. My one hobby, collecting tropical fish, was almost brought to an end that month when we woke up to find twenty-five dead fish, due to an imbalance in the water. Expenses came due for one of the children's college tuition. The air conditioning went out on my minivan, which is a necessity for me, and cost $1,300 to replace. Then my brakes failed which cost $600, and I hit a pothole, which cost more money.

Where was God now? He was right there, giving me the peace that passes all understanding and His sustaining grace (Philippians 4:7). He used these crises to give me the opportunity to fully share the gospel with the plumber, the two pet shop workers who tested my tank water, our neighbor who looked at our tractor, and the furnace installer.

From Bad to Worse

Then, on my way to help my son pick up something at Walmart, I slipped from my car door in the rain, and slammed my head onto the pavement. That caused a concussion and extreme dizziness for the next week and a half.

A week later, I fell into a sharp chair rail at church while standing to sing a worship song; it pierced my skin and spread my ribs. I covered my mouth to muffle my screaming as the church folks near me watched and cried. It caused such excruciating pain for the next couple of weeks that every time I moved my upper body to pull myself to stand, sit, or lay down I could hardly bear it. My mind was on the edge of insanity.

Within a week from that time, I was in the bathroom and fell against the scooter, hit the controls, went flying into the wall, and got catapulted into a wooden box. I blackened my eye, scraped my forehead, and messed up my neck again. But the trouble did not stop there—my passport renewal didn't come through so I had to cancel my flight to Canada where I was speaking in September. I ended up having to drive all the way there, which took about eleven hours.

After coming back from a grueling though successful trip (up until 2 a.m. every night for four nights in a row), I came back to the office only to stand up at my chair which rolled back and caused me to fall backwards and hit my head again. I got blood all over the carpet, but I cried out to God and He kept most of the dizziness away. I had to go to the chiropractor eight times and once to the emergency room during that couple of weeks.

Keeping Your Eyes Fixed on Jesus Christ

Through all that time, God hadn't abandoned me. He sustained me so I could keep working full time, teach government class to ten homeschool high schoolers, teach Bible class to five of my children, campaign for godly candidates, go to church, travel and speak, and survive each day. In fact, even though I've lost many of the great gains I originally had with the hyperbolic oxygen chamber, I'm now finally starting to regain some functions.

God is teaching me to look at a cup half full, not half empty. I believe that is the secret to keeping your eyes on Jesus Christ. We need to look for His cup of blessing in the midst of the pain.

What is Jesus Christ doing through this? We need to think and ask what opportunity is He making available to us so that we can glorify Him. We have to keep our eyes fixed on Jesus and as we do that we begin to see Jesus in all circumstances. We will be able to say that all things work together for good for those who love God, and work according to His purpose, and really believe it. He promises that He will give us the peace that passes all understanding; He tells us that as we "keep our eyes fixed on Jesus, we run that race with endurance." He says that we are to "take joy in our tribulations and trials" and revel in the fact that we've been included in the fellowship of His suffering.

The disciples rejoiced when they were stoned and beaten in the towns for the sake of Christ. Can we do any less? When we go through times of suffering, Satan attacks his hardest. He wants us to give up, he wants us to wait, he wants us to curse God, and he wants to neutralize us so we just focus on our problems.

But again we must put on the full armor of God and securely fasten the helmet of salvation, knowing that we are going to heaven and no one can stop us or snatch us from His hand. We need to mentally and spiritually put on the breastplate of righteousness against the whole world, and certainly against the bad circumstances that come our way. We must gird our loins with truth and not listen to Satan's lies telling us to give up, and think that we are nothing but a waste of flesh.

We have to keep our feet shod with the preparation of the gospel and be ready, in and out of season, to give a defense and tell of the hope that is within us. God makes it so clear: "How beautiful on the mountains are the feet of him who brings good news, who proclaims peace, who brings glad tidings of good things, who proclaims salvation, who says to Zion, 'Your God reigns!' " (Isaiah 52:7).

We must hold up the shield of faith, standing on God's truth, and thereby deflect Satan's fiery darts which he is sure to send our way. Finally, we must wield our sword, the Word of God, and cut through the trouble, horror, and despair, of the enemy before us (Ephesians 6:13–18).

Yes, we must keep our eyes fixed on Jesus Christ, but how do we do this? Let's look at the few examples I cited above.

How to Keep Your Eyes Fixed on Jesus Christ

When we got a leak and the plumber came out late at night, I had an opportunity to share the gospel with a stranger, and spent a half hour doing so. He received the Bible and the materials I gave him. I did not fix my eyes on the problem and the cost, but on what Jesus was doing in arranging a meeting.

When I fell, hit my head and got a concussion, I felt like throwing up and despairing but instead I prayed and tried to look for Jesus. I began speaking the Word of God, verse after verse, on my way to and from the CAT scan room and back to the downhearted nurse that was attending me. She ended up accepting Christ. God showed me this was really a divine missionary trip He had set up.

When I fell in my bathroom and blackened my eye, while I was lying on my back in great pain, I learned to say, "Blessed be the name of the Lord, you give and take away; blessed be your name." I found I could say this even though I was suffering and in pain. I had finally crossed the threshold of learning to praise God when physically there was nothing to praise Him about; it was like Paul and Silas when they praised God "in the midnight hour," chained in prison after a horrible beating. I praised Him with my heart even though my emotions were shattered.

As expense after expense came upon us, as material things broke down, from our car to our plumbing, it gave Him an opportunity to provide for us and help us to trust Him even more. And one by one, He has helped us to pay for many of the things in ways that I didn't anticipate. God was having me earn money in ways I didn't expect.

He held me up through the love of my incredible wife Tracy, faithful son Jesse, dependable son John, and my always loving and supporting daughters Bethany, Megan, Susanna, Charity and Amy.

Yes, God is with us—Emmanuel. He will never leave us nor forsake us. When we humble ourselves, He will lift us up (James 4:10). As I came to my wit's end in trying to determine how we were going to finance all these calamities, and how I was going to be able to survive all my falls, when

I needed my upper body to move and every movement, for weeks, was excruciatingly painful, God provided.

He rallied me once again. He enabled me to go to New Mexico from Sunday to Sunday and minister to many and be ministered to. He enabled me to speak and participate with the homeschool leaders, planning for legislation and to do mediation. He enabled me to make the flight and spend quality time with a lot of His people.

He enabled me at the "eleventh hour" to find an eighteen-year-old young man who was able to drive me to Canada, where we saw Niagara Falls on the way and had a great blessed time of ministry. He enabled me, through many tracts, to spread His gospel from New Mexico all the way up to Canada, through Maryland, Pennsylvania, and New York. He enabled me to share His truth in the hospital, which was a place I wasn't even planning on going.

There is one set of footprints left behind me—and they are not mine—they are my Father God's.

The Bottom Line

The bottom line is that He is showing, once again, that He is REAL, and He speaks loudly from *our* lives if we will only let Him. He gives the opportunity for us to be witnesses, if we only recognize it. He asks us to keep our eyes fixed on Jesus, not on our problems, so we can know true value and worth.

Ask, persevere, endure, and He will open a way. Praise God for His mercies that know no end.

Maranatha! Maranatha! Come quickly Lord, but in the meantime let us be faithful to our mission and be good Christian soldiers. Let us never give up. Let us trust Him and obey. And one day He will say, "Well done good and faithful servant." And all along the way He will give us sufficient grace, and through Him we can be more than conquerors because it is He who saved us. We can truly do all things through

Christ who strengthens us by fixing our eyes on Jesus. He is there and He will answer our cry.

I'm still here and He's still using me. You can count on Him doing the same for you no matter what the circumstance, no matter what the trouble, no matter how difficult it is. God is faithful and He is true to His Word. Praise His Holy name!

ARE YOU A MEMBER OF THE FELLOWSHIP OF HIS SUFFERING?

BEING AN AMBASSADOR FOR CHRIST

NOW THEN, WE ARE AMBASSADORS FOR CHRIST,
AS THOUGH GOD WERE PLEADING THROUGH US;
WE IMPLORE YOU ON CHRIST'S BEHALF,
BE RECONCILED TO GOD.
—2 CORINTHIANS 5:20

Most of us periodically go on vacations. It's an opportunity to rest, relax, and rejuvenate. It often can be a special time for you to have with your family or friends. But do you ever consider it as a perfect opportunity to serve as an ambassador for Jesus Christ?

The Bible states that we must be ready in season and out of season to give an answer to those who ask about the hope that is within us (1 Peter 3:15). The Scriptures make it clear that Jesus wants us to be not only followers of Him, but He has explained that we are to follow Him *and* He will make us fishers of men. There are no excuses found in Scripture that tell us that we can cease being a fisher of men when we are on vacation. There is nothing in Scripture that speaks of a rest from being a light that shines forth the truth of Jesus. Satan does not rest and relax—he is engaged in spiritual warfare for the souls of men 24/7. Why should we do any less?

There are passages that tell us we're not supposed to hide our light under a bushel (Matthew 5:14–16). Are we hiding our light under a bushel because we are on vacation and we are just thinking of ourselves? The opportunities we have to meet people who don't know the Lord are God ordained. He gives us these opportunities, I've come to realize, when we least expect it. So why not be ready?

Baltimore Getaway

One August, my wife and I had an opportunity to get away for two nights in Baltimore. We were blessed when we were at the North Carolina Homeschool Conference, with a gift from the homeschool group there. Since we were speaking at their conference on our twenty-third anniversary they gave us free Marriott reward points so we could stay anywhere we wanted for a couple of nights.

We set out for Baltimore from Virginia, and unfortunately got caught in horrible, rush hour traffic. Normally a one-and-a-half hour commute to Baltimore turned into a three-and-a-half-hour commute. We finally arrived in Baltimore in the dark, tired and hungry.

Conversation with the Bellman

While my wife was arranging for our room at the front desk, a bellman came out to the car to help us bring in our luggage. I began to strike up a conversation with him about his life.

I quickly learned that he had taken two jobs to provide for his family. One was at an office building where he said the people were stuck-up and looked down on him. Then he explained how much he enjoyed working as a bellman because people who came to the hotel were very kind to him.

I began to explain to him the hope that was within me and testified to him about God's sustaining power, giving him a little history of my own pilgrimage and a glimpse of some of the miracles I've seen God do on my behalf. He listened with all ears. By the time we were done, he was smiling and eager to hear more about the love of Jesus Christ. Later we left a tract for him and urged him to accept the Lord as his Savior.

A Late Night Chance to Witness in Front of McDonald's

After we brought our luggage into our room, we set out to look for a restaurant in downtown Baltimore. Downtown Baltimore on a weekday night is usually very serene and quiet. We found a restaurant and on the way back to the hotel, which was about five to seven blocks away, we spotted a McDonald's. My wife wanted to go inside and get ice cream, and I decided to wait on the scooter in front of McDonald's on the dark but well-lit streets. An African-American lady was standing on the same corner, obviously waiting for a ride. As I moved my scooter closer to her to begin a conversation, she moved a little further away.

As I sat there, thinking of how I could start a conversation, there was suddenly a noise behind me. Two overly cheerful men were dancing down the street, obviously high on something. One of them came up behind me and tapped me on the shoulder. As I turned to see who it was, I saw that they were harmless enough. I looked at the lady and rolled my eyes and she did the same.

I then began a conversation with her. Within no time, I found out that she was raised all her life in Baltimore and now she worked there and was engaged to be married. I brought up homeschooling. She readily identified with the need for a good education since the schools in Baltimore were so bad. She was fascinated with the possibility of homeschooling her future children.

As my wife came out, I said point blank to the lady, "Do you go to church around here?" She responded somewhat ashamedly, "No, but I should." And then I began to ask her more questions such as, "Are you a born-again Christian?" She said, "No, not yet." Then I told her how she could be born again by recounting the story of Nicodemus from John 3. I laid out the full gospel to her. She was grinning from ear to ear.

It was a chance encounter on a dark street corner in front of McDonald's, but it was God ordained to once again give me an opportunity to please Him by sharing the best news I could share.

A Change of Plans and an Evening Visit to the Baltimore Aquarium

The next day we had a relaxing time. We stayed in our hotel room until we went out to Walgreens and then a coffee shop where I was able to pass out two gospel tracts. That night, when we were headed towards the Bay where we were going for dinner, we noticed that the Baltimore Aquarium was open in the evening. So we opted to grab a quick bite, cancel our fancy dinner reservations and visit the Aquarium. After we were in the Aquarium for a while, which was fairly empty, we went over to an information desk to ask where the closest restroom was. As my wife went to use the restroom, I stayed by the information desk and began a little conversation with the lady.

"Do you like working here?"

She responded, "Oh yes! I love being able to talk about animals and biology with all the visitors. I'm a volunteer."

I said, "Wow! That is really sacrificial of you to give of your time to help people. I admire you for that."

After a little more chitchat, I asked her, "Do you go to church around here?"

She said, "No, I don't go to church."

Then I asked her if she believed in God. The lady replied, "No. I don't believe in God. I believe in forces out there that randomly moved and caused things to happen."

I had earlier asked her what she did for work and she said she was an eighth grade science teacher, so I was thinking she must have some pretty clear answers for what was the origin of the world.

I inquired, "Do you believe that there is intelligent design that created all these things since they are so complicated? Isn't it impossible for them to happen out of chance? Take for instance, the eyeball that is able to focus 10,000 different ways. This wasn't created by random force."

She responded, "I believe the forces come against each other and things are made, and the things that are worthwhile will last, and the things that aren't will not make it."

I looked at her incredulously because I thought she would have a much better answer, being a science teacher. At that point I just began to explain the gospel to her. I told her about John 3:16 and what Jesus did on the cross for her sins. I explained to her the power of God in my own life and how He had saved my twins' lives, and saved me from my multiple sclerosis month after month, year after year. As I gave her more and more Scripture, I began to see that it wasn't my words that would make a difference; it was God's Word.

My wife returned and I left the lady with a tract and urged her to turn to God. I said to her, "What if you're wrong?"

I knew that not everybody accepts the Lord when you share the gospel with them, but I also knew that His Word does not return void (Isaiah 55:11). Sometimes, just sowing seeds of doubt in their mind about their own "knowledge" is enough to get them to start seeking God.

I urged the lady to make a decision and left. Once again, God had turned an opportunity for vacation into an opportunity to be a missionary while on vacation. We did not even have to raise funds and travel to a third world country.

New Mexico Trip

Recently, my wife and four children and I went to New Mexico for a homeschool leadership conference. What an opportunity in the plane, in the airports, in the hotel, in the restaurants. On the plane, I sat across from a man with a blond ponytail and western clothes. I cheerfully exclaimed, "You must be from New Mexico!"

He said, "No, I'm from New Hampshire."

Oops. But we got into a lively conversation about his environmental job and homeschooling. Finally, I asked him if he knew where he was going if he died today. He responded, "I try not to think about it. I guess, nowhere."

I said, "What if you are wrong?"

At this point, he started to get silent. I just briefly told him what Jesus did on the cross. He then put in a movie on his laptop. When we landed, I gave him my own tract about the miracle of our twins' birth and how to be saved. On this trip, our family was able to proclaim Jesus by passing out tracts in many places around Albuquerque.

Don't waste your vacation on yourself. God is ready and willing to use you as a witness for Him. Remember we are to "make the most of every opportunity, because the days are evil" (Ephesians 5:16), and Jesus told his disciples, "the harvest is plentiful but the workers are few" (Matthew 9:37 NIV).

Let's make every day count for the Lord Jesus Christ. It is the least we can do.

CHAPTER
—— 1 3 ——

ONLY MOMENTARY LIGHT AFFLICTION

THIS LIFE IS NOTHING COMPARED TO GLORY!

FOR OUR LIGHT AFFLICTION, WHICH IS BUT FOR
A MOMENT, IS WORKING FOR US A FAR MORE
EXCEEDING AND ETERNAL WEIGHT OF GLORY, WHILE
WE DO NOT LOOK AT THE THINGS WHICH ARE SEEN,
BUT AT THE THINGS WHICH ARE NOT SEEN. FOR THE
THINGS WHICH ARE SEEN ARE TEMPORARY, BUT THE
THINGS WHICH ARE NOT SEEN ARE ETERNAL.
—2 CORINTHIANS 4:17–18

One year, from June to January, my multiple sclerosis became steadily worse. I am convinced it was triggered by both experimental and traditional MS medication that I finally tried after eight years of only nutritional remedies.

I became afflicted with chemical depression, sleeplessness, weak legs, a weak waist, a weak right hand and arm, a cloudy eye, a painful jaw, tremors throughout my body, a weak bladder, waves of weakness and fatigue, loss of balance (I fell twice a week), and many more symptoms. My MS was attacking almost every part of my body to some degree. For months, I literally wanted to die—heaven was all I could think about—all I could look forward to.

Yet God kept me going as I did the only thing I could—bury myself in the Word. I sang it, prayed it, spoke it, declared it, believed it, held on to its promises, and learned to trust Him more. There is power in His Word. I could not feel God, but I knew beyond all doubt, as I repeatedly declared and meditated on His Word, that He was there with me every step of the way. His Word reminded me that even though it felt like my MS symptoms would last forever, they were only temporary and light afflictions compared to eternity in heaven with my precious Savior (2 Corinthians 4:17–18).

I knew my feelings of hopelessness and depression were lies of Satan. God showed me that my battle was not against flesh and blood—it was a spiritual battle. He promised that if I resisted the devil, he would flee, "The angel of the Lord encamps all around those who fear Him" (Psalm 34:7). Also, just as God promised, the weaker I became, the stronger He was in my life. For years I had prayed, "Make me more like Jesus—whatever it takes." Now God was doing it; it was so wonderful, but it hurt so much.

In the two hospitals where I stayed, in May and November, God prompted me to give Bibles and tracts to scores of people and I personally shared the gospel with many of them. Two nurses, two cancer patients, and a hospital worker gave their heart to the Lord. One man I met in the Atlanta airport and another man I met in a restaurant in Texas were saved right before my eyes. Everywhere I go, then and now, I see God moving people by His Spirit in incredible ways. Through my weakness, His power has been displayed beyond anything I could have imagined. I cannot deny that God is using my MS for His glory to change lives. Satan's attacks are backfiring.

As God would have it, I still have not even missed any work (I just work more from my home office), so I can still direct the legal department and do all my legal, legislative, and international work. God continues to provide for my family and enables me to train my seven children in the midst of it. It is only by His mercy.

It was hard to have people praying for me and yet have no physical healing to report. Through everyone's prayers, though, God was graciously teaching me contentment and trust. He showed me that He did not need my strength or my courage. I truly lost most of my strength and all of my courage that year. He literally replaced my feeble strength and courage with His own!

God has reassured me that He has already ordained the days of use for my hands, legs, and the other functions of my body. Nothing I can do can extend their use. The worry and fear began to melt away as I realized I was in His almighty, sovereign and loving hands. It was not about me, it was about Him! Yes, even this seemingly never-ending and overwhelming trial was working together for my good and compared to eternity in heaven, this was simply a vapor! (James 4:14).

Then in the middle of January, as I got off the drugs, and the Lord led me into more new nutritional approaches, I began to gain many of my abilities back, little by little. My positive outlook returned, my hands, bladder, balance, and waist were restored in great measure, along with my eye and jaw. My independence was coming back. I was able to travel and speak in Seattle, Chicago, Wisconsin, and Memphis with more trips ahead. My stamina was high and I could exercise daily and swim strongly again.

Praise the Lord, for His mercies endure forever and His lovingkindness is everlasting.

I still struggle throughout every day. I cannot do many physical chores or activities with my family. But now I sing louder to the Lord because I went through a time when my tongue was becoming numb. I handwrite my prayers to God because I was losing the use of my hands. I stand for long times at church praising God because for a long time I could barely stand. I love my wife more and train my children more diligently because I was losing my will to live. I share the gospel and pass out tracts more boldly when I travel or do errands, because I did not think I would ever leave the house again.

God has helped me to work harder to make everyday count for the Lord. None of us knows how many days we have or how long our bodies will function. God is our refuge and strength, and even in the midst of trials that seem interminable we need to hold on to the promise of eternity where there will be no more pain and no more tears (Revelation 21:4).

We need to cling to His promise: "'My grace is sufficient for you, for power is perfected in weakness.' Most gladly, therefore, I will rather boast about my weaknesses, so that the power of Christ may dwell in me. Therefore, I am well content with weakness . . . with difficulties, for Christ's sake; for when I am weak, then I am strong" (2 Corinthians 12:9–10 NASB).

WITNESSING ON THE HIGHWAYS AND BYWAYS

BEING A BILLBOARD FOR JESUS

GO THEREFORE AND MAKE DISCIPLES OF ALL
THE NATIONS, BAPTIZING THEM IN THE NAME OF
THE FATHER AND OF THE SON AND OF THE HOLY
SPIRIT, TEACHING THEM TO OBSERVE ALL THINGS
THAT I HAVE COMMANDED YOU; AND LO, I AM WITH
YOU ALWAYS, EVEN TO THE END OF THE AGE.
—MATTHEW 28:19–20

Did you ever wonder when is it a good time to share the gospel with somebody?

Is it best when you have their full attention? Should we wait to talk to them when no one else is around? Should we set aside a few hours each week to go door-to-door, telling strangers about how to get to heaven? Should only full-time evangelists share the gospel?

The Bible makes it clear that sharing a message of our Savior and what He did on the cross is the most important news to share. The Bible also makes it clear that all of us have a responsibility to be ready to share the hope that is within us (1 Peter 3:15). Jesus himself said we are to follow Him and He will make us fishers of men (Mark 1:17).

The Bible refers to all of us as "ambassadors," that is, we are spokesmen for the Sovereign God of the universe, and He tells us, "How beautiful on the mountains are the feet of those who brings good news!" (Isaiah 52:7) So then, when do we share the gospel? And to whom? I think the answers are whenever we can and whomever is in our reach.

"Here, This Tells You How to Get to Heaven!"

Whenever I leave the house, I always try to remember to bring gospel tracts with me. Then as I travel on the "highways and byways" of life, I pass out tracts. When my children are with me, they join with me in passing out tracts. For example, whenever we go to the bank, we put a gospel tract in the container where we place our deposit in the drive-through. Or, if I am inside, the kids pass them out to customers going in and out. We explain to them that this tells them how to get to heaven. If we have to stop at various stores, we make sure we give tracts out in the store and to the clerks when we are checking out. I always ask a follow-up question of whether they know how to get to heaven. Many times they don't, so I tell them more or urge them to seriously read the tract.

"I Just Prayed Last Night"

When I was traveling with Megan and Tracy to Oklahoma City to speak at a homeschool convention, I met Brandon. He helped me get off the airplane by strapping me in an aisle chair and getting me to my scooter. At first this was kind of humiliating, but then I started looking forward to witnessing.

Later I saw him working as a skycap helping to load baggage that was coming off the conveyor belt. I secured his services and he proceeded to load our bags. I gave him a tract and told him that this showed him how to get to heaven. When I asked him if he knew how to get to heaven, he responded, "Not really." Brandon then explained that he was "not good enough." He confided to me that he was not living the way he should. I explained to him that all the good works in the world would not be able to save him. I told him that we are saved by grace alone and began quoting Scriptures that show that.

When I began sharing the hope that was in me, while we waited for our ride, he explained that just the night before, he got down on his knees and prayed to God that He would show himself to him. And now, he was amazed that he had met me. I responded that this meeting was ordained by God, and that God wanted him to follow Jesus. I gave him a tract and also a pocket Gideon New Testament Bible.

I showed him how to use the Bible index to look up various topics by page number. He was excited to get a bible that was small enough to bring to work in his pocket. I told him that he could ask Jesus into his heart tonight, and that he would be saved for all eternity. I explained that he needed to repent and give his life to Jesus Christ.

If I had kept my mouth shut or just talked about the weather, we would have missed this ordained meeting for me to help show Brandon the Way!

Is Anyone Ever Too Old to Accept the Lord?

When I was sitting on a plane flying from Dallas to Virginia, there was a lady sitting across from me in her seventies. She kept to herself and I smiled at her. I had read statistics saying that the older you are, the harder it is to accept the Lord—so, I admit, at first I thought "why bother?"

But then the Holy Spirit spurred me on and I began a conversation. I soon learned that she was heading to Oklahoma in order to minister to her daughter whose husband had been killed in car accident within the last few months. Her daughter had no children and had just gotten married. I did not know what to give her at first, besides verbal Scripture passages. But then I remembered that I had a copy of *Days of Praise* from ICR. So I asked her to give it to her daughter and told her that it would be a great encouragement to her. She was so thankful. She said she went to a Methodist church, but was still open to listening to the gospel.

The Friendly Airplane Steward

An airline steward, Jeff, helped me get on the plane. I began to explain to him about my MS, showing how God was carrying me and keeping me going, despite my decreasing physical abilities. I explained how God still gave me strength to provide for my family, all seven of my children and my wife. He was visibly interested so I showed him a picture of our family. My wife Tracy, my daughter Megan, and I all began a friendly conversation with Jeff.

During the plane's descent, I gave Jeff a copy of a tract that I had written, telling of the miracle of the birth of our twins and how God saved their lives. I told him it was like a *Reader's Digest* story. He was eager to accept it. I then asked him if he knew how to get to heaven and he responded "absolutely." When I asked him what he would say if God asked him why He should let him into heaven, Jeff said, "Because I am good." I then explained to him that we cannot get to heaven by works but only by grace and I shared some verses with him. We later learned that he lives fairly close to us in Virginia, and we are hoping to ask him to visit our church.

Going to the highways and byways of life is something we all do. We live in a free country where sharing the gospel is not a crime. We are told, "To whom much is given, from him much will be required" (Luke 12:48), and that God wants us to be "fishers of men" if we are going to be followers of

Him. We are *promised* that His Word will not return void: it will accomplish the purpose that God has for it (Isaiah 55:11). Therefore, we cannot lose as ambassadors for Jesus Christ. We shouldn't hold the good news in. May all of your feet be beautiful as you bring good news.

CRISIS EVANGELISM

YOUR ACCIDENT WAS NO ACCIDENT

FOR I KNOW THE PLANS I HAVE FOR YOU,
DECLARES THE LORD, PLANS FOR PEACE AND NOT
FOR EVIL, TO GIVE YOU A FUTURE AND A HOPE.
—JEREMIAH 29:11 ESV

One month four crises happened to me that God transformed into events of eternal value. God is teaching me that His ways are not my ways. I just need to be ready at all times to share the hope that is within me.

First, my son and I were driving to my chiropractor and I merged onto Route 50 from Route 28. As I pulled into the next lane, the traffic stopped but the Mack truck behind me didn't. Crunnnnnch! My back quarter panel was smashed, but the truck didn't have a mark on it. Needless to say, it was not fun sitting in my car, in the heat for an hour, getting weaker, and it has not been fun arguing with the trucker's insurance company ever since . . . but God had another plan.

A man named Gator came over to appraise my vehicle. He walked with a lift on his foot and had a shriveled leg. I found out he was in a bad motorcycle accident in which his friend was cut in half. I then had the opportunity for fifteen minutes to share the full gospel with him and he perked up hearing about the new bodies we will get in heaven! I called him back the next day and asked him if I could send him the story of the near death of my twins and how God saved them, and he agreed. He said he was thinking about what we talked about and anything I recommended for him to read "has gotta be good!"

I was in an accident so I could share with Gator.

Then our John Deere tractor died and our new neighbor, Wayne, came over. He has a cement company and works a lot with machinery. He heard the backfiring and said that my tractor was dead. Bummed out, I had it brought into the shop by a friend and found out it was actually fine. It just needed a new spark plug.

The next time I saw Wayne we had a good laugh, and then I asked him if he believed in God. He did, but he did not have a relationship with Jesus. I shared the gospel with him and invited him to church, and he said he would come.

I had tractor trouble so I had the opportunity to share the gospel with Wayne.

Then at 10 p.m., a pipe blew in our upstairs bathroom. Water was filling up the bathroom so I called a plumber's emergency number that I randomly found in the Yellow Pages.

Jeremy came over. He fixed the leak in fifteen minutes. Then, we began talking as I asked about his business. Within a few minutes, I asked him if he knew where he was going when he died. He said he did not, so I shared about fifteen verses with him on how to be saved as he kneeled by my feet. I gave him a Gideon Bible, a tract, and my twins' story.

Our pipe burst so I could share the gospel with Jeremy!

Recently, I was getting into my van at Walmart, it was raining and my grip slipped from the door and I slammed my head on the pavement. For thirty seconds I could not move or talk, and then the pain set in. I could not get up; when Jesse tried to help me up, my head spun and I wanted to pass out. Someone called an ambulance and I was whisked off to the emergency room. John rode in the back with me, and Jesse in the front. I testified about God's power to the medics, and then to the nurses at the hospital.

Then I went to get a CAT scan. The twenty-year-old nurse that helped me looked very despondent. I found out that she had been catapulted from a four-wheeler nine months before into a tree and had bleeding in the brain. She had been hospitalized for five days and was still having problems.

I started sharing the hope that was in me. I quoted many Scriptures to her and as each verse was shared, her countenance changed and brightened before my eyes. Than I prayed with her and she said she had goose bumps as she smiled from ear to ear. I told her, "God had me get in this accident so I could talk to you right now about your salvation." She immediately said with a smile "I know!"

I had my daughter Megan bring a Bible, the story about our twins, and a tract to the hospital when she picked me up. We looked for the nurse as Jesse wheeled me to the van. When we found her, she excitedly received my gifts. She commented that now she would have her own Bible to carry around in her pocket. When I asked her if she wanted to receive Christ, she said "Yes!" I also invited her to come to church with us sometime and she indicated that she would like that.

God turned a painful accident into an impromptu mission trip and saved a soul.

COUNT IT ALL JOY

OFFERING THE HIGHEST PRAISE WHEN WE SUFFER

YOU NUMBER MY WANDERINGS; PUT MY TEARS
INTO YOUR BOTTLE; ARE THEY NOT IN YOUR BOOK?
—PSALM 56:8

God is good all the time.

All the time, God is good.

God gives and takes away but my heart will choose to say, "Blessed be His name!"

In the midst of a difficult year, it was a truly wonderful blessing to see many friends at the national homeschool leadership conventions. It is like being with family. Somehow when I am with them, I seem to get a little better! God enabled me to drive back and forth to Maryland and Pennsylvania, rise up early and go to bed late seven days straight, participate in everything, have many meetings, and speak. He blessed me with a huge hug through all their encouragement to me!

My friends and their encouragements are such a gift, but the suffering I face every day is still with me. I need your prayers. Each year, I seem to lose a little more—my left big toe is now paralyzed and my dorsiflexion is increasing. I was fitted for another foot brace in hopes that it would help, but nothing can replace a lost muscle function. I lost the ability to go up stairs. My right hand can no longer type much or do many functions.

The Lord takes away . . . but blessed be His name! He is also giving to me! I have a most extraordinary and giving wife who won't quit even when the going gets tougher and tougher. He has given me seven faithful children who all love the Lord and who serve me in so many ways: praying, encouraging, giving me B-12 shots, stinging me with bees every other day,[1] strapping my feet on the stationary bike, helping me get dressed, getting my scooter in and out of our van— many things most kids never have to do for their dad.

Greatest of all, He lets me be a soldier in His service. I have the privilege of serving the homeschool community almost everywhere in many ways, even in my weakening condition. It is all from Him as He enables me to still run the HSLDA legal department, do radio interviews, write articles and columns, and speak.

Even though I have to go through a difficult life with MS, my suffering is actually praise when I triumph over the circumstances with God's strength and then bless Him in the midst of the trials. So often, when I'm struggling while traveling or functioning on a daily basis, God will turn around and bless me as I bless Him.

An example of this happened during my trip to speak in Dallas, Texas at a friend's convention. My daughter Megan

---

1. Actual stings from live bees. The Bee Lady (who also has MS) researched the benefits of bee sting therapy and came up with a protocol for applying the stings to various points along the spine and extremities.

and I took a taxi to the airport. The taxi driver, Abaas, was a Muslim and we had an intense forty-five minute talk about the Lord, ending with him gladly accepting a Gideon New Testament. At the airport, I talked for five minutes with the skycap and shared the gospel. God even kept the other travelers away. Amazingly there was no one in line—unheard of. We gave him a tract as we left.

In Dallas, we stopped at a gift shop and I gave a tract to the clerk. As I asked her if she knew where she was going when she died, she announced that she was a Buddhist. I shared God's Word with her. Then God gave me a great time of speaking and ministering to the homeschoolers at the convention.

On the trip home Saturday night, God continued opening doors but not exactly the way I wanted Him to! You see, I was weak from speaking and working all day. I had great difficulty getting on the plane. A flight attendant noticed my tie which had the Bible verse "I can do all things through Christ who strengthens me" on it. She said she was a Christian and encouraged me all the way to my seat.

Later, when I tried to get to the bathroom, I fell into the aisle. This was a night flight and most people were dozing— but not after I fell! I guess God wanted to get their attention because I sure had it. I was pulled to my feet and the flight attendants felt so bad for me that they put Megan and me in first class. As God would have it, I could witness to a different flight attendant all the way home.

When we landed, I was the last one off the plane so the pilot ended up helping me too. I shared the Lord with him. On the elevator I had another opportunity to share with a family who were traveling with their little boy with a broken leg. Then God ended the night by having us driven home by a taxi driver who was a Christian from Ghana. We praised God together all the way home singing hymns to the Ghana beat.

God takes care of the details doesn't He?

I am truly blessed. I need to keep counting it ALL joy, both the good and the bad.

GOD IS SOVEREIGN AND GOOD

THE KEY TO CONTENTMENT

O SOVEREIGN LORD, YOU HAVE BEGUN TO SHOW
TO YOUR SERVANT YOUR GREATNESS AND YOUR
STRONG HAND. FOR WHAT GOD IS THERE IN
HEAVEN OR ON EARTH WHO CAN DO THE DEEDS
AND MIGHTY WORKS YOU DO?
—DEUTERONOMY 3:24 NIV

As, year-by-year, I descend further into the handicapped world, the Lord is teaching me to have more and more patience and contentment—with less and less. It sounds bad, but I can wholeheartedly say along with Joseph, "God meant it for good" (Genesis 50:20). I know His promise is true that, "All things (even MS) work together for good for those who love God and are called according to His purpose" (Romans 8:28). I am learning to fully trust that God *is* sovereign, and that is my security. He is in control, even when events seem out of control. I am also learning to understand and have compassion on so many hurting people as I tread down the same paths that they must walk.

I have had falls that have injured my back, knees, elbows, and almost every part of my body. I can now relate to the sufferings of people with partially and fully paralyzed limbs (my feet and right hand, legs, and waist are mostly paralyzed), and the people who experience pain in their joints, and those who have bladder and bowel issues. And I understand the spiritual attacks against you when you are physically weak, and the feeling of despair and depression. That doesn't count the normal stuff like teen issues, relationship challenges, financial hurdles, car and home repairs, a busy full-time work load, job pressures and obstacles to overcome, changing churches, and the pressure of teaching two homeschool classes to eighteen kids.

All this, God has ordained for me and He has given me nothing that I cannot bear with His constant, sustaining power and grace. I find, too, that I can comfort those who are suffering with the comfort God has given me. I can better understand their hurt and pain and sorrow.

I have become a dependent. I can now understand how dependent people feel; and I can appreciate their suffering, pray more effectively for them, and love them. Because of my ever-increasing handicaps, I know what it is like to constantly battle feelings of inadequacy, rejection, loneliness in suffering, being a burden on others, having others argue over who has to help you, not being able go anywhere alone, being dependent on a scooter and batteries to move, and the frustration that you are trapped in a body that won't do what you want it to.

Of course, when you're handicapped you have to painfully face the realization of what you can no longer do with and for your wife and children. You have a thousand funerals in your mind for all those activities that are dead to you—activities like not being able to play catch, stand and balance, play Ping-Pong, write with your right hand, dribble a ball, shoot hoops, hit a baseball, go caving, go hiking, skip a rock in a stream, wash a car or floor, cut your own food, put in your own contacts, button your shirt, clean a closet, open the door for your wife, camp out, throw a football, shoot a bow or slingshot, take out the garbage, paint a porch or room, change the oil, mow your lawn, prune a tree, cast a fishing rod, carry a suitcase, climb stairs, lay on the beach, get off the ground by yourself, swim normally, walk more than a hundred steps, walk holding your wife's or child's hand, dance with your wife—the list seems endless.

Through it all, God has shown me that He is far bigger than all that. I know now, more than ever that, "The Lord will guide you *always*; he will satisfy your needs in a sun-scorched land" (Isaiah 58:11 NIV). He answers my cries to Him; He always is with me, and keeps all my tears in a bottle. And the greatest thing He gives me is himself. What a loving God!

He takes my weakness and makes me strong. I see Him change my speaking ministry from normal to Holy Spirit powerful. Scores of people come up to me at every conference and speak of how the Lord is convicting them and changing them right there, helping them to serve and praise Him more, love Him more, love their wife and children more, be more sold-out for Jesus, trust Him more, repent of sin or give their life to Him.

Every time I speak at conferences, witness to strangers, teach in my classes, or share in family devotions, I feel His pleasure. It is awesome. I am soaring high on eagle's wings—yet my body scrapes along the rocky ground like a heavy anchor. I so yearn to be a spirit and leave this body behind, "I trust in you, O LORD; I say, 'You are my God.' My times are in your hands" (Psalm 31:14–15).

I yearn, like Paul, to be absent from this body and present with the Lord, for that is far better. But as Paul said, "to remain on in the flesh is more necessary for your sake" (Philippians 1:24 NASB). God has a mission for me and for each of us. We cannot leave until we have accomplished the mission. He will give you and me the right equipment to finish.

When I cried out for healing, He gave me more grace. And the grace was always sufficient, "I will refresh the weary and satisfy the faint" (Jeremiah 31:25 NIV).

I cried out for ability, and He gave me a scooter that re-opened my life and an Endless Pool where I can swim thirty laps and exercise nearly every body part like crazy, even ones I can hardly move on land. God has enabled me to do this four times each week, and to work out with weights in the middle of the night or early morning.

When my strength failed, He reminded me that, "I can do all things through Christ who strengthens me" (Philippians 4:13). I am still able to work full time, provide for my family, teach homeschool high school classes twice a week, direct the HSLDA legal staff, be a husband, swim thirty laps, supervise a garden in our yard on my scooter, solve a lot of problems, and with my wife, train our seven kids. It is all God's faithfulness—for my strength is gone.

As I have said before, when you look behind me these last five years or so, there is only one set of footprints and they are NOT mine. My Father God is lovingly carrying me!

Since March of 2009, God has enabled me to speak in Florida, Utah, Nebraska, Colorado, and Massachusetts, ministering, in His name, to thousands. At the hotels, in planes, to Mormons and to Muslims, all over, I have been able to witness the gospel to many individuals. It has been such a comfort to rely on the promise that God is sovereign and He is in control of each and every circumstance I find myself in. This is easy to believe in the good times, but not so easy in the hard times. I must continually speak His Word to myself when I'm in those hard times and remind myself that, "all things work together for good" (Romans 8:28).

I will end with still another miracle, where God has shown me once again that He is real and answers prayer. When I was invited to speak in Florida, I decided to take the whole family and make the trip into a vacation for a week. God graciously provided a condo, a van, and tickets to the parks—all for free. It is little blessings like this in the midst of the physical trials that remind me that I have a loving heavenly Father who cares for His son.

BOAST ABOUT YOUR WEAKNESS

GLORIFY YOUR SAVIOR

FIGHT THE GOOD FIGHT OF FAITH, LAY HOLD ON
ETERNAL LIFE, TO WHICH YOU WERE ALSO CALLED
AND HAVE CONFESSED THE GOOD CONFESSION IN
THE PRESENCE OF MANY WITNESSES.

—1 TIMOTHY 6:12

God is good all the time. All the time, God is good. I believe that with all my heart—but my flesh still hurts.

As I grow weaker, God's power is displayed in greater ways. No doubt about it. God's promises are true! "May it never be that I would boast except in the cross of our Lord Jesus Christ, through which the world has been crucified to me, and I to the world" (Galatians 6:14 NASB). So I will boast about the cross of Christ wherever I go.

When I speak at state homeschool conventions, I can feel His pleasure. The Holy Spirit literally gives me the words to speak. This year I have already spoken to at least 15,000 people. In Indiana, my PowerPoint presentation failed before a crowd of 3,000, so I gave an altered talk without notes. I was overwhelmed as people came up to me after the presentation and I saw that God had changed so many hearts in so many ways. In Michigan, before 2,500 people, with no projector for my PowerPoint, I gave, at the last minute, a new keynote address without notes—I had no nervousness; there was no weakness as I stood, no stumbling. I was able to tell many stories of God's deliverance of homeschool families, warn of apathy, and fully share the precious gospel.

In Wisconsin, again with no notes, a heavy speaking schedule at the state conference, preaching at my parents' church, and speaking on a national radio program, again lives were changed. With a weak body—it was all God, as I somehow managed to keep on going. In Richmond, there was the same effect as I spoke to individuals and to thousands. People wept as I spoke. The Holy Spirit empowered me and moved the audiences. I shared the gospel to thousands of students' relatives at a graduation. God is giving me boldness to speak His truth like never before. I talk about the need for faithful fathers and husbands, close communion with God, the dangers of virtual charter schools, diligently teaching our children about the Lord, not giving in to Satan's temptations, scores of stories of sacrifice and freedom. I can't hold it in!

"My grace is sufficient for you; for power is perfected in weakness." Most gladly, therefore, I will rather boast about my weaknesses, so that the power of Christ may dwell in me. Therefore, I am well content with weaknesses, with insults, with distresses, with persecutions, with difficulties, for Christ's sake. For when I am weak, then I am strong.

—2 Corinthians 12:9–10 NASB

Last year, I felt like giving up traveling—it was just becoming too hard. But on the plane, I looked up and God gave me a vision of Jesus motioning me with His hand to keep on going. Now I better understand why He gave me that picture of His Son.

The hard part about MS is the constant fluctuations between feeling good and feeling horrible. The bee stings from the live bee sting therapy gave me quite a good jolt—my strength increased. In fact, I was doing about ten stings every other day, sticking strictly to my healthy diet, weightlifting, stationary biking, and doing leg exercises for two hours everyday. Then I had three falls in rapid succession. I believe God is working, but my flesh is still hurting.

One evening, I was leaving my house to teach at AWANAs and I fell backwards onto a wooden foot stool, hitting my elbow on a shelf, and smashing the stool with my back, right where my kidneys are located. I could not speak at first or move my legs at all—the pain was too intense. My daughter was with me and I cried out for God's mercy and prayed that I hadn't damaged my kidney. My family called 911 as I crammed some tracts in my pocket. God was arranging another sudden missionary trip.

An ambulance came and a paramedic asked my name. When he heard it, he said, "I know you! I'm a homeschooler and joined HSLDA." God put me right at ease. I testified to both of the paramedics about God's power to heal and save. At the hospital, I was able to share the gospel with three others and give them tracts. God healed my kidney that night—x-rays showed that it was okay. I still had pain for the next four weeks, however. "But He knows the way that I take, when He has tested me, I shall come forth as gold" (Job 23:10).

A week later, I was driving down our street on my scooter with my seven-year-old son John on his bike; we were laughing and circling each other and going in and out of driveways. Then I turned at top speed on an incline and got thrown from the scooter, landing on the same elbow I had hit on the shelf when I fell on the stool the week before. I lay in the middle of the street unable to get up. Then, as I prayed, a motorcycle and a car came up. Two "angels" lifted me up on my scooter. I was able to drive home.

The following week, I was riding my stationary bike too vigorously and lost my balance. I slammed down on the wood floor still strapped onto the bike and hit the same elbow again. My family pulled me up, and by the Holy Spirit's power, I resumed biking. That same week, in a freak accident, I hit my eye with a falling cane and got the biggest black eye I ever had!

Yet God has kept all my bones from being broken as angels cushioned the blows; they held me and lifted me up for, "The angel of the LORD encamps all around those who fear Him" (Psalm 34:7). In the midst of all the physical testing, the spiritual battles have intensified as well. During the time I was writing one of my books and speaking, I could feel the spiritual war waging around me. Satan wants to take me down, no doubt about it. I wrestle regularly with him and chase him away in Jesus' name. I am learning to put on my spiritual armor every day. I have learned that my battle is *not* against flesh and blood, but against spiritual forces of evil in the heavenly places that we cannot see with our eyes (Ephesians 6:12). It is so clear to me now.

I do not want to live if I can't give. God has heard my cries and deep groaning over my gradual losses. He blesses me with seven wonderful helpers that I can train, teach, and love in return. I always travel with one of them now and our time together is so meaningful, so filled with learning experiences and opportunities to serve, plus they see God working up close. They help me pass out tracts and witness to strangers on planes and hotels. What a wife God has given me. Tracy is a wonderful way that God, my Father, demonstrates His unconditional love to me. There are no words to describe what she means to me, and no words can explain her loyal and selfless love.

Am I blessed? Without question. God gives me full-time employment at the best job in the world, and it is work for His people. He uses me to give, although I have nothing of myself to give. Wow! He is teaching me to boast in my weaknesses (2 Corinthians 12:5, 9), fight the good fight (1 Timothy 6:12), and press on towards the goal (Philippians 3:14). I am running my race, though it might be on a scooter, and in such a way that I might obtain the prize (1 Corinthians 9:24). Even though boasting in your weakness might seem pointless, we need to remember that it is when we are weak that we are truly strong (2 Corinthians 12:10).

I want to thank each of you for your selfless love and prayers for me and my family.

God is good all the time! All the time, God is good!

One thing I do, forgetting what lies behind and reaching forward to what lies ahead. I press on toward the goal for the prize of the upward call of God in Christ Jesus.

—Philippians 3:13–14 NASB

BETTER IS ONE DAY IN YOUR COURTS

LOOKING FORWARD TO THAT DAY

CAST YOUR BURDEN ON THE LORD, AND HE
SHALL SUSTAIN YOU; HE SHALL NEVER PERMIT
THE RIGHTEOUS TO BE MOVED.
—PSALM 55:22

Chris had planned this chapter, but was unable to finish it. We have decided to leave it as is, as a gentle reminder that all that we think and plan is in the hands of our Father in Heaven. He is in control.

THE JOURNEY HOME

COLORADO SPRINGS, COLORADO
SEPTEMBER 20 – OCTOBER 12, 2009

**From The National Home School Leadership Conference
to the Hospital**

Recollections of Chris Klicka, by Dennis Alberson

It is a privilege to talk about my time with Chris during the last days of his life here on this temporary home. I call it that, because Chris *was* ready to go to his true "home."

Our friendship had grown over the past few years through the homeschool venue. In April 2008, Chris spoke at our state homeschool convention in New Mexico where he gave the address for the graduation. It was truly special for my wife and I as our oldest daughter Courtney was graduating.

After the convention, Chris and three of his children joined us for a few days to visit some sites in southern New Mexico—Chris shared with me that he knew he would not be able to do many more of these outings. Toward the end of our time together we had a wonderful time of sharing and praying. We laughed, we cried, and we spent wonderful hours together.

It was then that I got to see a side of Chris that truly touched my heart. It was a deep, deep love for his wife Tracy and his children; it was only surpassed by his love for his Savior. He expressed a genuine concern for their well being when he would be gone. He knew that the Lord would provide for all his family's needs, but like all men, I guess, sometimes our egos come into play. We feel that since we provide leadership for our families and for their spiritual, physical, and mental needs, we wonder who God will use in our absence? Much more was talked about and prayed over. Then suddenly in our silence, Chris cried out, "Lord, take me home; I'm ready when you are." The battle was wearing hard on our warrior Chris.

Chris's message through the years has been made powerful because of his battle with multiple sclerosis. Many times Chris had shared with me that he was tired, beaten down, and not up to the task at hand. But, time and again, the Lord in His faithfulness gave Chris not only the strength to go on, but to go on powerfully! Chris stated many times that the message he shared was perfected through his weakness. Had it not been for his illness, his will and his desires might have been manifested by his own efforts and strength, rather than fully relying on God's power.

During Chris's attendance at his last National Homeschool Leadership Conference in Colorado Springs in September 2009, God's power was even more evident. Chris had been quite ill leading up to the conference, and I didn't expect that he would be able to attend. Imagine my delight when I walked into the hotel and found Chris in the lobby sitting there on his scooter, smiling. I had not spoken to him in weeks, and I was elated to see him. The look in Chris's eyes always spoke volumes. Those of you who knew Chris know what I'm talking about. His love for his fellow man never wavered.

It was evident at the start of the conference on Sunday evening that Chris was fighting the battle, but defeat was beginning to surface. Chris talked about his inability to work, and that he probably needed to consider going on full-time disability with HSLDA. In previous conversations, Chris and I had talked extensively about how MS affected many of his body functions, temperature regulation being one of them. Since January, Chris had been battling hypothermia (subnormal body temperature), which is rare in MS patients. He was finding that his baseline temperature was going lower and lower and was now hovering around 93 degrees. Anything lower than that was increasingly debilitating.

On Monday morning, Tracy, who knew Chris might need some help with his bowels, found an excellent hospital in the area and was preparing to take him in for a procedure to have him cleaned out, and sure enough, Chris did need some help. So that afternoon Jesse helped his mom get Chris to the ER, and after an outpatient procedure he felt better, but was pretty weak. Because of this, Tracy called my wife, Cathey, and told her that she could use some help bringing Chris back to the hotel for the conference.

By the time we got to the hospital Chris seemed to have new energy, and interestingly enough, just as we were ready to start loading Chris into the van a snowstorm started. No, not a storm, it was more like a blizzard; wind was blowing and there was snow everywhere and all over us. The snow didn't seem to bother Chris at all; in fact, back at the hotel he commented on how much better he felt. He had an appetite and ate well at dinner.

On Tuesday, Tracy had to fly to North Carolina to be with their son John for a few days, and as Chris and I had lunch together he commented on how much better he felt and that he had more energy than he'd had for days. He also mentioned that he hadn't been sleeping well because he couldn't seem to get his brain to slow down. It was like one thing after another just kept coming to his mind, and there seemed to be so many things that needed to be done.

It was noisy in the dining room and Chris told me again how difficult it was to hear; I had noticed that at times he didn't respond when people stopped and talked to him.

As we were sitting there, suddenly he said with concern, "Something is just not right. I don't know what it is, but something isn't right!" Tracy had only been gone a little while and he was already missing her. Chris also mentioned his concern for his seventeen-year-old son, Jesse, who had a lot on his plate and he wanted him to make good, godly decisions during this season of his life.

He admitted that he knew people were speaking to him at the conference, but many times he didn't respond, and he said that it bothered him that he couldn't hear them. Chris stopped and uttered, "I just want to be held." I wrapped my arms around him and held him. Through tears we began to pray and Chris lifted up his family, his life, his work, his associates and then he quoted from Psalm 23, "The Lord is my Shepherd, I shall not want. He makes me lie down in green pastures; He leads me beside still waters. He restores my soul. He leads me beside still waters. I shall not want."

I had my guitar, so I begin to play and Chris closed his eyes and sang along; "Blessed Be Your Name," "Amazing Grace," "Be Still and Know," "There's Just Something about That Name." The Lord was faithful and settled Chris's spirit. Time had gotten away from us and we had missed supper, but my lovely wife thought to bring us some salads and we dined in style in Chris's room.

At the Wednesday morning session the next day, I found out that Chris hadn't slept well. He felt like he hadn't slept at all. He seemed very unsettled, and his spirit was restless. He appeared less responsive to people speaking to him and his movements and speech seemed difficult. Again he stated, "Something is just not right!" We stopped in the back of the meeting room, I put my arm around him and we prayed. At this point, very "unlike" Chris, he was unable to pray, but he was grateful for my prayer.

The board for The Alliance Conference (which took place during the first part of the week) had asked Chris to lead the prayer for the noon meal. Chris wanted to pray even though communication was difficult for him. His spirit was willing, but his body was weak. He was able to ask the blessing, but it took great effort, with long pauses.

The chef at the hotel, aware of Chris's special dietary needs, had gone out of his way to help him. He came by and checked on Chris and prepared wonderful dishes for him, but for lunch Chris said, "I'd like a salad." The wait staff brought Chris a cooked beet and spinach plate and his look was priceless as he said, "I'd really just like a salad." Our waiter, thinking that a fish dish would be good, brought a plate of broiled salmon and vegetables. Again, Chris's look was priceless, "I'd really just like a salad." We did finally get a salad, but Chris had difficulty getting the food on his fork. I set my fork on his plate and kind of pushed the food onto his fork. Chris, still having a sense of humor, smirked and called me a "pusher."

Thursday morning came and Mike Donnelly asked Chris if he was up for speaking at the presentation. Trying to be helpful, he graciously informed Chris that when the time came for him to speak, he could share as much or as little as he liked. As the morning progressed things got more difficult for Chris. He was unable to speak well but wanted to press on—always the fighter, never giving up. On the way to the morning workshop I watched Chris as he was unable to respond to any of the people that spoke to him.

During one of our earlier conversations Chris told me that he had a digital thermometer that he used regularly to check his temperature because of his continual hypothermia. He had been unable to get a reading earlier on Thursday, so we agreed to try again. We attempted several times unsuccessfully to get his temperature. When we did finally get a very low reading of 91 degrees, Cathey and I were not confident that it was accurate.

When lunch was over and we were heading back to the room, we realized that the sun was shining—the Lord had provided a beautiful day. I suggested to Chris that we go outside since I knew how much he enjoyed "soaking up some vitamin D" and he agreed. I positioned Chris outside in the warm sunshine and left to get him some water. While I was gone, Chris decided to take off his coat all by himself. Mind you, this was the same guy who couldn't lift his fork the hour before. Only God could do that!

We returned to the hotel and Chris was ready to go to his room. Once again, for thirty minutes, he tried to use the bathroom, but to no avail. We then sat in the room and started talking about everything that was going on inside his body. Chris became extremely unsettled at this point and cried out, "Why God? What is going on? What is it you want from me? I'm ready to go home." Tears were shed and again Chris said, "I just want to be held." I wrapped my arms around him and held him and began to pray, and I could feel Chris lean his head onto my shoulder as he wept. We prayed for awhile and the Holy Spirit came, and a peace settled over the room. We praised God.

On Friday morning, Chris came to morning devotions a little late. He seemed to be having trouble holding himself up on his scooter. Speaking was extremely difficult for him that morning; again he had not slept well. He was scheduled to participate in another session with Mike Donnelly later that morning and Mike checked in with Chris and encouraged him to speak whenever he liked; and if not, that was okay too.

Chris was unable to navigate the scooter; he had trouble lifting his hand at all. He asked, "When will Tracy be here?" as Tracy was scheduled to fly in early Friday evening. Unbeknownst to me, Leah, Chris's legal assistant had called Tracy that morning and asked her if we should get Chris to the hospital or wait until she got there, she replied, "Get him in right away!" Tracy discovered that she could get on an earlier flight into Colorado Springs. She walked to the gate and because of Chris's condition, was permitted to get on the plane even though it was just ten minutes before departure.

At the conference, Chris was unable to speak at all during the session with Mike. They cut the session short so we could spend time praying for Chris. What a glorious blessing to hear the heartfelt prayers of the saints!

After this, Dr. Dobson was to be awarded a lifetime achievement plaque. I asked, "Chris, would you like to go hear Dr. Dobson speak, or do we need to take care of Chris, and take Chris to the hospital?" I was not sure what his answer would be, but he decidedly replied, "Chris!"

When we arrived at the hospital, the medical staff took us to a waiting area and tried to get vitals on Chris. I told the triage nurse that we were unable to get a good temperature reading because of his low body temperature. A few minutes later when she was unable to get a temperature reading, she informed us they would try again later when Chris got an ER room.

We waited another thirty minutes. I asked the male nurse to check Chris's temperature. The nurse started to use an ear scope, but I suggested that it might not work, and it didn't. Chris's temperature was too low.

At St. Francis Medical Center, the Flight for Life helicopter was grounded, and the nurse that worked on the helicopter was filling in at the ER. The Lord was at work. The ER doctor came in and I explained Chris's situation to him and asked him if we could get a temperature reading as it might be part of the problem. There was no comment from the doctor, but he started ordering tests and scans.

The doctor left, then out of the blue, George Klicka, Chris's dad called to check on Chris. I let him know the situation and held up the phone to Chris's ear and upon hearing his dad's voice he tried to speak. A little conversation transpired, but then Chris couldn't speak anymore. I told Mr. Klicka what was happening and he said to me, "You know, if his temperature gets too low, he's gonna have symptoms like that."

I told him that I had mentioned it to the medical staff three times and, as of yet, we still did not have a reading, but praise the Lord, the Flight for Life nurse was listening and said, "We need to get a core temp reading on Chris." So, because of Chris's difficulty urinating, they opted for a catheter, and they had one with a temperature probe imbedded in it.

They discovered that Chris's temperature was a critically low 85.6 degrees (a patient can go into an irreversible coma at 86 degrees). The doctor immediately ordered a warming blanket that would raise Chris's temperature slowly so as to not send his body into shock, and within the hour, Chris showed signs of improvement and began to comprehend some of what was going on.

One thing that I'll never forget happened on Monday when I was preparing to leave, I was with Chris, and I asked him if I could pray for him. He said yes, but when I was finished praying, I saw that he was praying for me. He was praying a blessing over me! God's power was still being perfected, even through Chris's weakened state. Praise God!

Recollections of Chris Klicka, by Cathey Alberson

Oh, the sweetness of seeing my brother in Christ again. After Chris's health struggles earlier in 2009, it amazed me to see that he had made the trip to the National Homeschool Leadership Conference. I shouldn't have been surprised, however, as Chris was a fighter. Chris and my husband Dennis connected right away and they enjoyed watching our kids while they were catching up. Chris mentioned his frustration with his recent therapies not seeming to help, but ended with, "God is good . . . all the time."

During the conference when Chris had trouble speaking, I was encouraged that Dennis seemed to understand how

Chris felt and what he was trying to communicate. Both Dennis and I were continually amazed at how Chris tried to "keep on keeping on." Chris's joy at being surrounded by his larger national homeschool family thrilled my heart. Once again, *God is good . . . all the time!*

When Chris was unable to speak at his Thursday morning session, I grieved for him, but looking back see how God provided an opportunity during that workshop for the body of Christ to stop and pray for Chris. And later when it seemed that Chris needed to rest, God helped him perk up enough to join us for the family outing to the Garden of the Gods. God blessed us with a gorgeous afternoon—on what would be his last day out. *God is good . . . all the time.*

Even though he wasn't feeling good on Friday morning, Chris insisted on going to the session where he was supposed to speak. As the morning progressed and Chris got worse, unable to speak at his session, even then, he seemed to try to press on. When Dr. Dobson was scheduled to speak at the luncheon, Chris, who normally would have done everything in his power to be there (Tracy told me so), knew he needed to go to the hospital. With tears in Chris's eyes, Dennis and I went into action to get him to the hospital right away. The road ahead was going to be tough, yet *God is good . . . all the time.*

Chris had spoken many times of how blessed and humbled he was to be moved and carried around. He related it to how the men carried the crippled man and lowered him down through the roof to Jesus. Now, the Lord provided the extra man power needed to get Chris in the car to take him to St. Francis Medical Center ER.

While waiting in the ER, Chris's eyes would brighten when someone he knew came to see him, and even though his temperature was a drastically low 85.6 degrees, he still tried to keep up a cheerful spirit. He wasn't always able to speak and often couldn't smile, but his eyes would brighten and he usually could pull off a side grin. When Tracy arrived later that afternoon Chris seemed much more at peace. Again, *God is good . . . all the time.*

The next morning, on Saturday, September 26, Tracy and I arrived at the ICU to find Chris's temperature had risen to a dangerously high 97 degrees. Still below normal for the rest of us, but for Chris with his MS, it was like having a temperature of 105! Tracy and I went to work to help Chris by pulling off his blankets, unplugging the warming machine, getting cool, wet rags, and turning Chris so that he could breathe as he was becoming paralyzed by his high temperature. The nurses in the ER weren't aware of Chris's needs like Tracy was because she had been monitoring his temperature for years, especially since he had developed hypothermia in January.

Bridgett, his ER nurse, became very concerned because his vitals had plummeted (heart rate, blood pressure, and oxygen). I remember praying over Chris, and once Bridgett asked me if he had more family. She stayed on top of his condition and worked closely with the doctor. Tracy noticed that Chris wasn't improving after an hour of being on medication and actually seemed worse. She asked if he might be reacting negatively to the medicine they had given him, and they agreed to try another one.

Within thirty minutes, his blood pressure began to rise a little, a blessing from the Lord. At every positive change in numbers on the screen I would say "Praise God." Bridgett stayed with Chris for another hour as his condition remained fragile. The doctor came in several times and once stayed for thirty minutes while they assessed what to do next to keep Chris alive. His blood pressure was up, but his oxygen levels were still low so they put an oxygen mask over his face. Because he didn't respond quickly enough, they came very close to putting him on a ventilator. Tracy told the doctor that she and Chris had, months earlier, discussed ventilators and that he didn't want this procedure done. She replied, "I know he doesn't want this done, but if it comes to needing one, I'm overruling Chris in this case; I have the power of attorney and this is about saving his life!"

The doctor wanted to know if family members were nearby. He told us we needed to get them there; Chris was "critically ill," and there was a good chance he wouldn't make it through the night. Those were tough words to hear, but God provided the power and strength we needed as we prepared our hearts for the journey ahead. So our prayer became that all the kids could make it in to see their dad. We also prayed that George and Ardie, his parents, would be able to see their only child one more time. We had faith and we trusted in our Lord to provide.

HSLDA had changed the evening plan for the conference in order to have a tribute to Chris, and Tracy planned to sing for this tribute. By Saturday evening Chris's vitals were stabilized, but he was still in critical condition. Tracy felt led, however, to go to the banquet and sing, something Chris always enjoyed hearing her do. Tracy, and the girls and I went to the banquet.

Meanwhile, Dennis was picking up John at the Colorado Springs airport. Our good friend Eugene Like from New Mexico was picking up Bethany and Megan at the Denver airport, and it was amazing to see how God brought the whole family together and how they comforted one another. After being with their daddy for awhile, they all went to the waiting room, except for Amy. Sweet little Amy stood there caressing her daddy's hand and just watched him. She then shared stories with me, of her and her daddy. There's no doubt in my mind that Chris heard every word and was blessed to listen to the love in Amy's voice when she spoke of her daddy. Up until this point, Chris had not been responsive. Just then, Amy's eyes lit up as she said, "He squeezed my hand! He squeezed my hand!" The Lord had provided Chris with strength to live a little longer. *God is good . . . all the time.*

George and Ardie, Chris's parents, arrived the next morning. By this time, Chris was more alert and his vitals were looking good. The waiting room continued to be filled with believers praying for Chris. We knew how important relationships were to Chris, so we let in as many friends as he was able to receive. His most treasured moments were with his family. Several times his girls were with their dad and would sing to him. Once they sang, "Great Is Thy Faithfulness." After they left Chris said, "Ah, my angels."

Once, after the girls had left, Chris looked at me and said, "I'm ready; take it out." I responded, "Take what out?" With expressive eyes and a slight smirk he replied, "You know what. Now take it out." "Okay, Chris, I'll see what I can do." Well, he was right. I did know what he was asking me to take out; I just couldn't tell him that. Chris had had a central line put in the day before when the doctors and nurses were working to keep him alive. Now that his parents had made it and all his kids were there and Chris was out of immediate danger, that line wasn't needed. Taking the line out, however, meant he wouldn't have it if his vitals took another dive, and they probably wouldn't be able to get it in quickly enough to help him. If that happened, it would likely be the end for Chris.

The Lord is the Alpha and Omega, the beginning and end, so Chris's end was in the Lord's hands. Knowing Chris's wish to not be kept alive with machines, he was asking that it be removed and was trusting that God was in control. The decision was made to remove the line, and afterwards, when I returned to the room, Chris said, "Thank you; you're a blessing. I'm ready." I could have argued with Chris that, no, I was being blessed and he was the blessing, but I had learned you don't argue with this lawyer; just do as he asks.

Later, John flew back to North Carolina to continue filming *Hero*. By Sunday night Chris was the top performer of the ICU and was promoted to the fifth floor. Once he was there, Chris was okay but very confused. He kept saying he wanted to go home. He didn't want to be in the hospital. Tracy gently replied to him, "You and I are husband and wife. We are one, and together we make a home. Wherever you and I are together is *home*." Chris gave that little grin to her and we left the two of them together at their home in the hospital room. All that night, Tracy and Megan stayed in the hospital room with Chris to make sure he was never alone. *God is good . . . all the time.*

On Monday, September 28, Chris had a busy day with many people coming to sing and pray or just visit. Among the visits was a phone call from his friend Joni Eareckson Tada. Chris smiled after speaking with her and they both agreed to dance together in heaven someday. Joni asked how she could pray for Chris and he said, "To finish strong!"

This day also included lots of time with the family. Megan would often read Scripture to Chris. Jesse had some time with his dad, and of course Chris received numerous hugs from his girls. Once, while talking with Megan and Bethany, he mentioned he had not finished this book; he had only one more chapter to write. Megan replied, "Don't worry Dad; we'll make sure your book gets finished." "That would be good," he responded.

Chris and Bethany were talking about heaven and going through the list of great Christians that he would soon be seeing in heaven. He was pretty excited about getting to heaven, but while the Lord still had him here, he was eager to be with his family as much as possible.

That night Bethany and I agreed to stay with Chris. After such a busy day, we thought he would sleep well, but we were wrong. Chris had many things on his mind that night and kept calling for me. He was speaking of heaven and would tell me things I needed to tell Jesse. He wanted to know when John would be back. He would quote parts of Scripture, phrases from songs, and then give instructions to me.

One instruction was that I tell the nurses who gave him a bath, thank you. "Also, tell them that was like what Jesus did before He died; he washed the feet of his disciples. That was a loving thing for them to do for me," he said. Chris was always thinking of others. After five or six hours of telling me things, he then asked for Bethany, so I woke her up. Chris had more things to talk about. Her soft, peaceful voice was so reassuring and comforting. It was precious to hear her finish her dad's thoughts, since it took awhile for Chris to get out all the words. Despite his condition, he never once complained. His mind and heart were focused on the last few laps, not on himself. This was evidence of his prayer being answered, "To finish strong."

On Tuesday morning Chris awoke for some visits, but was a little tired—imagine that! This was also the day we transitioned Chris from the hospital to hospice care at Stan and LeAnn John's home. What a tremendous testimony of God's provision for Chris's last few laps. The family was blessed to be together and in a loving Christian home.

As Tracy and I were preparing Chris to travel via ambulance, I asked how many could ride with him. The answer was, "None." That was not an option for Tracy. To move him that way would cause more confusion, so I told them Chris wouldn't be going if Tracy could not ride with him. Once again God provided, and they allowed Tracy to ride with Chris to the John's house where a room was set up for him that had a beautiful view of Pike's Peak. Chris was very pleased to be out of the hospital and into a home with his family. *God is good . . . all the time.*

On Wednesday morning, September 30, two hospice nurses arrived early and after checking him out, determined that Chris was not in good shape; his lungs had started to fill with fluid. I learned later that these same nurses were so touched by Chris's family and the testimony of Chris's life that they went outside together, after their visit with Chris, and prayed that he would live until John could return to Colorado later that morning.

John arrived that morning to see his dad, and Chris once again had peace now that he was there. Psalm 29:11 says, "The Lord gives strength to his people; the Lord blesses His people with peace." We arranged the bed so John could get up with his dad. Later that afternoon, everyone gathered for a time of praise and worship. Chris's joy overflowed! What more could a man ask for than to be together with his family praising the Lord in his last few days?

Megan had previously contacted one of her dad's childhood friends, Eric Vouga. On Wednesday morning, he and another high school buddy, Jim Blair, got on a plane and traveled out to see Chris at the last minute. They arrived that afternoon to find Chris feeling and doing much better. God gave him an amazing amount of energy and he visited and laughed with these two men for two and a half hours! Once again, even though Chris was ready for the finish line, the Lord provided a blessing for him and his friends.

During the next week and a half there were many ups and downs. Chris's condition would worsen, and he would come within inches of the finish line and then the Lord would give him the strength to carry on for a few more days. It was evident that the Lord was working in every moment and that God would answer Chris's prayer to "finish strong." Once when I gave Chris some water to drink on a sponge, he said, "Delicious! Thank you for not giving me vinegar. You know that's what they gave Christ?"

Chris was an incredibly gracious patient. He needed to be moved regularly, from side to side and up in the bed. Bob and I would tease Chris about being too tall and Chris always gave a comment or smirk in response. At one point Ben Arnoldbik, Bethany's husband, was there with me, and Chris asked for some weights so he could exercise. We looked at each other as if to say, "You have got to be kidding me." I had learned not to question Chris, however, but just found some weights for him. Ben stayed there with Chris while he "worked out." That afternoon was his last workout.

We continued to have worship times with Chris. It always brought peace to Chris to worship the Lord. Even when he was unable to make sounds to sing, Chris was moving his lips and singing his heart out to the Lord. Once while I was sitting with Chris in his last days, he said, "My heart . . . my heart . . . will choose to say . . . blessed be the name of the Lord."

On Monday, October 12, we—Tracy, the kids, Bob Farewell, and I—were all there at the Johns' home, but in different parts of the house. Tracy and the hospice nurse and I were in the room with Chris, who was unconscious and unresponsive, when we noticed his breathing had changed. The nurse told Tracy to bring the kids in to see their dad; he didn't have much time. Very quickly, all the kids came. Tracy was praying for Chris, encouraging him to run into the arms of Jesus. When the last child came in, Bethany said, "Okay, Daddy, we're all here." And just like that, Chris took one last breath and that was the end. The ones who meant the most to Chris, his family, were all there. God had answered his prayer to finish strong; great is Thy faithfulness. And yes, *God is good . . . all the time.*

Hospice Care to Homecoming

My Special Last Visit with Chris Klicka, by Beth Raley

I have had the privilege of walking with the Klicka family through these past few years of Chris's multiple sclerosis. Having been as close as one can be to the situation, though still not being in it, has allowed me to hear often of Chris's struggle between flesh and spirit. In his last days he described the growing struggle between wanting to remain on this earth with his beautiful family and wanting to serve his heavenly Father by answering the call to go home.

On October 4, 2009, one of his last Sundays on this earth, he continued to fight the fight between flesh and spirit. In his flesh he wanted his family to be by his side that morning, but in his spirit he knew that it would be best for them to attend a local fellowship to worship with other believers. Chris had spent the day before wanting to talk to Tracy to tell her how much he loved her, how much she had meant to him over the years, and how much he valued her as the perfect helper for him in his life, both in sickness and in health.

This particular morning, Chris struggled with the fact that Tracy was able to go to church with the children while he was unable to do so. Chris wanted his family in church even though he wasn't able to attend with them. He said, "I know this has been very hard on them too." So, with Tracy and the children joining the John family at their church that morning, I felt God's leading and was given Tracy's grateful permission to stay with Chris.

As Tracy's best friend, I am grateful for the events of that morning with Chris. Chris and Tracy had been one for over twenty-five years; growing in closeness and unity, in sickness and in health, committed to walking in Christ's love until death would part them. And now the parting seemed close at hand. The last few years had been difficult for both of them, but they were together through it all. Now it clearly seemed that God was ordaining separate paths for them, albeit separate only by location. God was calling one to continue life here on earth, and one to start life united with Him in heaven.

They had both been feeling the pain of being torn apart since their paths had been diverging, but nothing compared with this week when their final separation appeared imminent. Chris talked about wanting to stay by Tracy's side; I reassured him that Tracy wanted the same, but that the Lord was ordaining a journey for both of them. It would still be with Him, but they would be separated from one another. Chris would be going into death alone, without her, and she would be going on with life alone, without him. Neither of them, however, would ever be without Christ. He responded that he "was lonely" as he experienced the beginning of this separation process. I reminded him that Tracy's journey, without her beloved Chris, was lonely too. They would only find comfort in knowing that Jesus was there with them, and was with the other on their journey.

Chris described that he was "sad and glad," sad to leave his family, but simultaneously glad to soon be rid of his "broken body and the pain of this world." The depth of his honesty moved me and we continued to talk at length about how no one except Tracy felt this sadness and gladness like he did.

She has known the pain and difficulty of Chris having to "keep on keeping on" for months and even years; she stepped in for his body as his body increasingly let him down. Chris's body had not even been able to regulate its temperature since January and Tracy had been there putting blankets on him, getting him warm tea, taking clothes off him, and getting him ice water, depending on his fluctuating needs. She had been repeatedly taking his temperature to monitor it so that he was comfortable and could move and even survive. Now, even with close monitoring, his body was not responding to the external efforts to maintain his body temperature. Chris said that he felt that he was "making a transition."

I strongly encouraged him to have all the conversations he wanted to have with Tracy because it was possible he would not be able to talk the next day. I wanted to be sure he wasn't surprised or felt trapped by his body but that he used his mouth while he could, to say the things that he wanted to say to his family and friends. I also wanted them to have the conversations they felt they needed so that they didn't feel cheated out of that time with Chris.

Chris told me again that he loved Tracy and the children and that he wanted to stay with them, but he knew he couldn't. The day before he thought he had told Tracy this, but he had not. He reminded me of all the cards that he had sent to her over the years and how he had always tried to let her know how much he loved her. As his MS progressed, he tried to give her some space, knowing how difficult it was for her to care for him and homeschool. He commented that he was struggling more and more to stay awake, and I told him that possibly, one time soon, he just wouldn't wake up, or at least not to be able to talk. I urged him to take this opportunity to talk while he had it.

After the family got home from church, I spent some time trying to facilitate communication, but since Chris was having a spiritually difficult day it seemed fruitless to everyone. I was afraid of what might be ahead, conversations planned but left unspoken. Tracy and I discussed this, and she made herself available to Chris throughout the day, but that talk just did not happen. Before Tracy and I went to bed that night, Tracy prayed aloud with me, "Dear Lord, if there is a conversation that you, Lord, feel needs to take place, we pray that you would supernaturally get me into the room so that it can happen."

The next morning, Monday, Chris did not wake up. He never opened his eyes; he never made a groan; he didn't even stir but slept peacefully with rhythmical breathing that seemed would last forever. Reflecting on his burst of energy on Friday, followed by paralysis of his legs on Saturday and total paralysis of his physical body on Sunday, leaving him with only his ability to talk, my fears of his being unable to talk on Monday seemed to be realized. At 10:00 that morning while Tracy and I were in the kitchen getting tea, Tracy looked up in tears and said, "I wish someone would have told me." My heart ached, like a shot went through it because I knew how much Tracy wanted to have that last conversation with Chris. She looked at me and asked, "You did tell me, didn't you?" I didn't respond, but only prayed that the Lord would allow more time for them if He deemed that best.

In the previous week, Tracy and the children had given many hugs and kisses to Chris. "I love you" had been spoken to him countless times, and many tender times of caring for Chris took place since he had gone into hospice. Each of them had spent some wonderful time alone with Chris, and Tracy had lain down beside Chris on several occasions, just to be near him and comfort him. In addition, being all together in the John's home had given the younger four children opportunities to tell Chris good-bye. They had told their dad they loved him and that it was okay for him to go to be with Jesus, that they would be okay because God was taking care of them.

That day they left to spend a couple of days at a friend's ranch as the days ahead would be difficult. Jesse was invited to go to the ranch as well, but he decided to stay with his dad, along with his mom. The day passed with Chris in a state of unconsciousness. We continued to check on him, tried to rouse him and talk to him, but all day long it was only one-way communication. He did not take any liquids. He did not move his head. He did not squeeze any hands. That night at dinner we were missing Chris already.

After dinner, as we sat in the family room around the fire, I thought it might be a good time to call a friend who had wanted to sing a song to Chris over the phone. Just before 8:00 p.m., I went up and told him that someone wanted to sing to him. He immediately opened his eyes and said, "Hi! Been a hard day." This startled me and I called for Tracy and Jesse, knowing that if Chris was conscious again he needed to be talking to them instead of me. They came running to his side and had a brief interaction with Chris before he fell asleep.

Once again, we all gathered in the family room. After about a half an hour, while we were still savoring those moments with Chris, we heard someone bellow out, "Hey Tracy!" This time everyone was startled, and somewhat confused, until we saw Tracy leap up saying, "That's Chris!" and ran to be by his side. There she sat for the next few hours with her beloved Chris. Knowing her prayer from the night before, I was amazed at God's gracious answer. I shared with the others that Tracy had prayed that God would "supernaturally get her into the room." From the man who had not spoken a word all day and who had only spoken with a whisper for the previous few days, we all could see that his clear, loud shout to Tracy was "supernatural."

It was 11:00 p.m. and time for bed, but trying to get Chris to settle down now when he had not been able to share his thoughts for over twenty-four hours seemed impossible. Everyone went to bed while Jesse remained by Chris's side, sleeping on the cot next to him. Chris continued to talk into the early hours of the morning.

At 4:00 a.m. Jesse, who had been unable to get any sleep through the night, traded places with Tracy. She tried to help Chris settle down so they could both get some sleep. When this didn't work, Tracy, feeling exhausted, asked me to go in with Chris. I attempted to reassure him that everything would be okay, and we could talk later in the morning. To this, Chris lifted himself up off the bed, looked me right in the eye and said, "Okay? Okay? Do you think this is easy? I'm dying. This isn't easy; it's hard." At that moment it was clear to me he was completely lucid and needed to talk. Waiting until later in the morning was not the solution.

I realized how trite my comment had sounded. I told him I was sorry, that I knew it couldn't be easy and that he was absolutely right; he had no time to wait until later for anything that he wanted to say. I told him that he needed to have any conversation he wanted to have now while he still could, because if this was his last opportunity he didn't want to miss it. He responded, "You got a point there," and then continued. "I have a plan for Jesse and need to talk to him about it sometime." He told me he had a combination of books in mind that he wanted Jesse to read. He wanted to talk to him about learning "how to drywall, doing basic fix-it stuff. I've already spent some time doing this." He wanted to tell him that "he needs to respect his mother and help her."

In the midst of this conversation about Jesse, Chris interspersed plans for himself to address his MS issues. It seemed that as he was speaking of all that he wanted to tell Jesse and all that he wanted Jesse to know, he started to wonder, as any parent would, how this could possibly be accomplished if he was not here to do it. Chris had expressed many times his great love for his wife and family and the difficulty that he was experiencing in leaving them. However, each time he also knew that Jesus Christ was active in each of their lives and that Christ himself would continue to minister to them in Chris's absence.

Chris further shared with me how he had such great assurance that Ben would take excellent care of Bethany. He told me, "Ben is a very good man. He is wise and strong. I know that he will love my Bethany and appreciate her, like a real man." He also said that Brendan would be a "great husband for Megan. She needs someone strong. I think he will be good for her." He told me many times what a wonderful mother Tracy was and that he knew, without a doubt, that she would continue to be there for the children, loving them and nurturing them in the admonition of the Lord.

In the case of Jesse, however, who was so close to manhood yet still needed to learn more about how to be a man, it seemed more difficult for Chris to trust that God would provide this guidance in his absence. Chris realized that he was in the process of handing over the mantle to the next generation, his children. He was trying to adequately describe it to me and trust I would communicate it to them.

I decided not to wake Jesse, but reassured Chris that I was writing down everything he was saying to share with Jesse later, in case Chris wasn't able to say these things himself. As we conversed early that Tuesday morning, Chris needed a few reminders to stay on track with what he felt was most important. The Lord was kind and gave him another opportunity to say everything he wanted to say. Chris went on, "All right, two different levels, one getting MS, the other a charter." Chris continued to express his desire for Jesse to know how to take care of a house, realizing that one day he would be responsible for his own home. I assured Chris that the Lord had provided Jesse with men who would come alongside him to teach him these things, and that knowing practical skills was important, but hearing Chris's heart now was more important. I said, "Anyone can teach Jesse how to take care of a house," and Chris replied, "Right, right, I see what you mean."

He then shifted the conversation back to times when he and Jesse had talked about getting ready to live his adult Christian life. He had talked to Jesse about having godly relationships with girls and to guard his heart. He went on to describe boundaries that he had set for Jesse, in order to protect him, and to talk about his desires for Jesse. He said to me, "I've done probably one thousand hours of time with him. I've prayed one thousand prayers. I've cried one thousand tears for my son."

Chris also told me how proud he was of his son. He told me how close he and Jesse had become over the years. Chris remembered how he would take Jesse to conferences even when he was young and his son would help at the HSLDA booth selling books. He said he could always count on Jesse "to do what he was supposed to do." He said, "Everyone else could see it too. They always commented on what a good boy Jesse was and how much he honored his Father through his service to me, even before the MS got so bad." He told me how Jesse would sit on his lap for hours and they would just talk or he would tell him stories. He remembered how Jesse's only thought was to please his dad.

Now, Chris was leaving behind a teenager who was in the midst of trying to figure out for himself what it is to be a man and how to please his heavenly Father. Chris seemed to be finding it difficult to trust God with the magnitude of this issue. God can be trusted with our lives and the lives of those we love—the lives of our children, even our teenagers.

I shared with Chris that death was not the end, particularly for the believer in Christ Jesus. The Lord works through our sufferings and will use even death to draw people to himself and conform those whom He loves to the likeness of Christ.

Chris said he wanted to stay in the race, but he knew he couldn't, so he wanted to "finish well." I told Chris that he had run the race well, and that he had trusted Jesus in the easy times as well as in the most difficult times—with this being the most difficult of them all.

Chris told me, "I have endured afflictions, shared the gospel and ministered to families whenever the Lord has allowed me to do this." He went on to say, "I have fought a good fight, I have kept the faith."

Chris reminded me that for fifteen years he had been seeing himself become physically weaker and weaker. He lamented that MS had taken so much from him, yet he continued to serve and he gave me many numbers—numbers of families he had worked with, numbers of lawyers he had worked with, numbers of states and countries that he had spoken in, and with it all, trying to carry on the work that he felt had been prepared for him by the Lord.

He said, "I'm not trying to be forgetful but there is transition. I've got to get dressed, got to get going, people are calling. I've been sleeping longer; I've been walking with God longer. I need to get to the office. I am off and need to minister to my family. Jesse is the one I've poured my doggone life into.

"You know what else I did? I witnessed to our chiropractor and he became a Christian. I'm not driving anymore; Jesse drives and comes with me to the chiropractor whether he wants to or not. When we are alone, he's done a lot, but there is more he can do, as far as love, loving others." Chris seemed to have periodic concerns about leaving things undone, of wanting to do more, or in his own words, to "keep on keeping on."

Earlier in the week Chris was delighted when Megan read Hebrews 11 to him, the Hall of Faith, which starts out, "Now faith is the substance of things hoped for, the evidence of things not seen." These verses were shared with him to encourage him, and seemed to have their intended effect. God was faithful to minister His Word to Chris.

Because I was taking notes as Chris spoke, I asked him if there was anything specific that he wanted me to write down and pass on. At that point he changed from a conversational tone to one of dictation. It was as if he were giving a formal presentation complete with facial expressions and dramatic inflections. He proceeded by sharing the following:

"I know this—God is sovereign and He loves me.

"I know this—before the foundation of the earth, He made me in the hands of 'the perfect God' according to His purpose.

"So it's okay. I *want* to stay in the race. I *want* to be eighty years old. I *want* to be there.

"But I can also say this, it's hard to descend and lose body parts and functions. You know I've lost a lot. You know, I used to be a big weight lifter. Now I'm not a big weight lifter. What I do now is little ones."

(Chris spoke of the covenant between Tracy and himself.)

"I had to give up my wife physically. I've given that up; I've had to.

"I've had to give up buttons, putting on my shoes.

"I've had to drink my green drinks, faithfully, every day. Green drinks! Does it stop the MS? Noooo!

"It's the praises, the praises to God. He's gotten me through this." (Chris looked up to the sky and squinted and stared.)

"I really, really have no fear."

Chris's conversation continued until Jesse got there. As he talked with Jesse, Chris needed reminders as to what he had wanted to say to him. Some of his comments got a bit mixed up like when he told Jesse in a very serious tone, "It is better to be a strong man than a weak woman." This caused Chris to chuckle as he realized how it had come out. He added, "I didn't mean to say that." The Lord's kindness and mercies were evident even in this most sober of situations.

Periodically Chris asked, "What else did I say?" to which I read from my notes and he replied, "Yeah, yeah, that's right," and then went on completing his thoughts. Eventually Chris's conversation drifted into hallucinations, tangential comments and conversations with people we could not see. From that time on, Chris spent the day with bright eyes fixed on things beyond. He seemed to be focusing, talking and responding as if in conversation, but the conversation had nothing to do with any of us.

Tracy and I planned for my departure on Friday. When Friday came, it was extremely difficult for me to leave, but I had the strong sense that these next few days were exclusively for the family. It was time for me to go.

The Lord had provided Bethany with stand-by tickets so that she could get to Colorado Saturday morning. With Bethany already there, Megan was prompted to fly out that afternoon and arrived late Saturday evening. As a result, the entire family was back in Colorado Springs together, sharing more kisses and hugs and "I love you's" with their dad.

It was not until Monday morning at 11:00 that I learned of Chris's final breath—Bethany and Megan were back in Colorado by his side with Tracy and the rest of the children. The beauty of His plan became so clear to me. I prayed with sorrow and with gratitude; "He doeth all things well."

Thoughts on Chris's Last Two Weeks on Earth, by Stan and LeAnn John

> Precious in the sight of the LORD is the death of His godly ones.
>
> —Psalm 116:15

Chris, what are you looking at? What do you see? Oh, how I wished I could get a momentary glimpse of the heavenly scene into which Chris was peering. Frequently, his countenance of awe, like a young child seeing fireworks for the first time, would cause all of us to long to catch a glance of our own. Chris, can you describe the wonders being revealed? Shhh, truly the Lord is near!

The Lord was always truly near to Chris Klicka. It was evident that he had developed a skill in battling the disease that had sought his life these many years. The skills of resistance, the strength to carry on, now carried Chris far beyond any expectation of those providing him tender care. We were seeing the same resilience that had enabled this godly warrior to achieve so much on the behalf of millions. Now, it was providing time for one more conversation with a family member, or a visit and encouragement to a childhood buddy. Chris was not going to let go, not until things were complete. And through it all, while slipping in and out of our presence, there was a dialog of what we could only conclude as prayer on Chris's lips. It was not a "new" prayer, but the familiar prayer of one who was accustomed to being in the presence of God. It was not articulate speech, but we all knew we were party to a heavenly conversation. Shhh, truly the Lord is near!

"I'm hungry." Words clearly spoken by a man who had not eaten solid food in five days! Now he was ready, and determined. There was a little scramble, discussion of what might be best, and *voilà*, a meal. Chris responded, after taking a bite of scrambled egg, "This is bland. Do you have any spice . . . cayenne?"

I replied, "Oh, LeAnn doesn't think that would be good on your empty system."

"Is she a nurse?" Chris countered.

Determined, taking hold of the zest of life to the end, Chris continued to amaze us all. And yes, he enjoyed the spiced up meals that were happily prepared by the many loving hands gathered to serve the man who had served them so well. Fellowship, laughter, tears, service, and songs of worship were spontaneously produced by the love that permeated the air. Shhh, truly the Lord is near!

In the bustle of the coming and going of many friends and admirers, times with Chris were few. Occasion was typically found in the quiet hours when the family withdrew for time together and exhaustion had taken its toll on others. Reading from the Psalms and sometimes singing, we would do our feeble best to minister to Chris. One day after I had read a couple of Psalms, I sang a song from Psalm 27:4 and then Isaiah 40:11. When I had finished singing, Chris plainly said, "Amen. Dear Lord, we give You all the glory. We don't know what we are doing day by day, but You give us hope." Shhh, truly the Lord is near!

In his final hours here on earth, I never heard Chris mention anything about work or the other things that brought him on this impossible last mission of service to the home-schoolers he loved. As his physical strength waned, Chris focused on the two things dearest to him. His first focus was on praising the Lord and seeking His face. At one of those times, his daughter Megan asked Chris what he would like us to sing. Chris quickly and confidently responded, "Great Is Thy Faithfulness." As we sang, Chris feebly breathed the words right along with us with an evident belief in the words he sang. Though he could barely speak, he would ask about Tracy and the children. Simply being told where they were and what they were doing, he would nod in the satisfaction of knowing that they were well, and drift back to sleep. Love for God and love for family . . . life's best treasure. Shhh, truly the Lord is near!

One last time with family, and Chris slipped into the arms of his Savior. Precious in the sight of the Lord is the death of His godly ones (Psalm 116:15). Now we know why . . . they reveal God's face to all who are near.

Thanks, Chris for showing us Jesus! Good-bye, we will see you again one day soon for we know where you have gone. Peace, the Lord is near.

November 30, 2009

Looking Back on My Journey with Chris at the End of His Life, by Bob Farewell

The memorial service is over. The crowds of people paying respects to the family have all gone home. Even the daily activities of family life of the departed have resumed their normal course. But I am missing my friend.

For the better part of twenty years, this vivacious, ingenious, and courageous defender of parents to homeschool their children has been a faithful friend to me and my family. We often found ourselves participating as speakers and exhibitors at homeschool conventions, he representing Home School Legal Defense Association, and our family representing Lifetime Books and Gifts.

Part of the dynamics of participating in these homeschool conventions is the opportunity to share your life with the many attendees, as well as create strong friendships with the other "road warriors" who travel the convention circuit. Over time, Chris Klicka became one of my best friends. If either of us had a spare moment or there was a lull in the convention hall, we would seek each other out to share our challenges and accomplishments with each other.

But more often, than for any other reason, we invariably found ways to bring humor to each of our lives. Humor was our hook for each other. It was what brightened our day. It was our way to share joy with each other and with those around us. It was a pleasure to make each other laugh, even through the hard times. And hard times for Chris were a constant companion. We would call each other to share a story and wind up praying for one another. Chris always found a way to bring our focus back to our Savior, Jesus Christ.

It has been tough to watch my friend become weaker and weaker with his MS. Being a "fix-it" kind of guy, I found myself sad and frustrated. For the last year of his life we talked to each other by phone almost every week. It became harder and harder to find humor to lighten our hearts, but we did . . . all the way up to his passing into Glory.

This is how I saw Chris complete his life. My good friend Chris ended his life strong; he did indeed finish well.

About a month before the National Homeschool Leadership Conference, scheduled in Colorado Springs toward the end of September, 2009, Chris called me one Friday night. His voice was almost unrecognizable; the MS had progressed so much it impaired his ability to speak. Chris began to tell me good-bye. For almost an hour, he and I cried over the phone as he explained that he had reached his end. He had fought MS for fifteen years and was now tired and ready to go home to his Lord and Savior.

Chris said he was not attending the conference, not taking any more speaking opportunities, and resigning his position at HSLDA to go on full-time disability—and was praying the Lord would finally take him home. This tearful good-bye would not be our last, however. Just two days later Chris called me to say he had changed his mind—he was not going to quit HSLDA, and was hoping to attend the National Leadership Conference the following month. I was dumbfounded, but shared his optimism and said I looked forward to seeing him in Colorado Springs surrounded by over 400 special homeschool friends.

When I walked into the front door of the conference hotel, I found Chris riding through the lobby; he made his way to me. He looked extremely tired and had difficulty pronouncing certain familiar words. I was so concerned for his condition I asked him, "Are you on medication? I can hardly understand you!" Chris replied, "I guess I'm just too tired and I need some HUMOR!" Little did I know how badly we would both need our special hook of humor in the days ahead.

By week's end, Chris was admitted to St. Francis Medical Center's Intensive Care Unit. After several tense days there, he was moved to a private home under hospice care. Stan and LeAnn John opened their home to Chris and often as many as twenty other friends and relations. At times we could almost feel the intensity of the thousands of prayers that were prayed for Chris and his family while there in Chris's bedroom.

During his stay at St. Francis, I was struck with the idea that someone needed to record what was happening and what was spoken to and by Chris. I am a speaker by profession yet a reluctant writer. I had just purchased a personal Daytimer, however, and had brought it along for this trip. So I wrote down what I witnessed; soon it became a labor of love.

For the next seventeen days I found myself writing down most of the interchanges that took place between Chris and his family and friends. Of the nearly sixty edited pages of notes I recorded, some too personal to share publicly, many of the things Chris said and did impacted me in a big way.

On one occasion, I was moved by how concerned Chris was for his family's well-being. He knew he was dying, yet he still felt the burden of responsibility for the care of his family. He said to us at his bedside, "Look, I only have two weeks left before my next paycheck. I have seven kids to feed and I have lots of work to do." We responded that his family's needs were covered and he just needed to prepare his heart to rest in the Lord.

I particularly loved watching Chris delight in singing songs of praise and worship when friends stopped by to visit. Here was my friend, who could hold an audience spellbound for over an hour, struggling with his uncooperative lips and voice—all the while smiling as he tried to sing along.

On several occasions I would hold a cell phone up to his lips as he would speak to various friends and relatives. Often I was moved to tears as these dear friends would pray for God's blessing on Chris and his family and he would just sigh an "Amen."

Even in his sleep late into the night Chris would call out, "In Jesus Name, in Jesus Name!" Oh, how I loved his love for the Lord.

Later as his life was nearly gone, Chris moved from a semi-conscious state to being wide awake for a few minutes, and then back again. Friends sang to him, prayed for him, and stroked his arms and hands. He lay still for many hours.

One day, while semi-conscious, Chris kept trying to speak. For hours he tried to make words, but we could not understand what he tried to say. He appeared to have animated conversations with whomever he saw in his dream-like state. Suddenly, Chris opened his eyes and turned his head toward me. Speaking in a loud voice, he said, "Bob! Bob! Is that you? Are you dead too?"

Rather taken aback, I responded, "No, brother, I'm not dead yet."

Then, in his next breath, he said, "Can you believe I love you?"

I replied, "Yes, brother. I love you too."

This was my highest and best moment. I believe Chris was dreaming about others he knew who have died and was speaking to them in his dream. When he woke up and saw me next to him, he thought I might be dead also.

Chris's non-verbal communication touched me deeply. Though at times we thought he was unaware of our presence, he'd surprise us by doing something to let us know he was listening. Whenever Tracy put her face close to her beloved Chris's and say, "Where's my kiss?," Chris would purse his lips to give and receive a kiss of affection. As I stroked his face, I teased him that his face felt "rather flinty." He pushed his unshaven cheek out with his tongue. When the family gathered around his bed for a photograph, Chris mustered a big smile. Other times he smiled with just one half of his face. We all laughed at his antics. Chris just loved to laugh and have others share his joy.

The day before Chris passed into Glory, he remained in a state of semi-consciousness, but would respond occasionally. Our hostess, LeAnn John, softly sang a song of praise to him and at the end, Chris responded "Amen."

Later, Chris prayed his last prayer aloud, but very haltingly, "Dear Lord, we give you all the glory. We don't know what we are doing day by day—but you give us hope . . . and we ask. . . ."

While still semi-conscious, Chris raised his left arm upwards and out to the left of his body and stated, "Beautiful!" Moments later, Chris spoke in loud voice, "Hello out there . . . Chris Klicka here!"

Then, the last words I recorded . . . "This is it!"

My hardest moments were when the funeral home van arrived to transport the "empty body-house" of my friend to their facility. Remembering how much Chris loved to share the gospel with total strangers by passing out gospel tracts, I was inspired by a friend's idea to share his joy of the Lord in one last special way.

I placed one of Chris's gospel tracts into his lifeless hands and folded them over his heart. We could only imagine the surprise and hopefully, delight that would have been experienced by the person receiving his remains. I can hear Chris laughing in my mind every time I remember this event. He would have loved it!

The seventeen days I spent at the bedside of my friend, Chris Klicka, will forever be a part of what makes me who I am. I feel a sense of privilege to have been there with Chris and with his entire family during Chris's final journey. It was through God's providence that I was able to stay for the duration. Witnessing the strong faith of my dying friend has made my walk with the Lord that much richer.

I will miss you, my friend, but never will I forget you.

About the "Scribes"

Dennis and Cathey Alberson

Chris met Dennis and Cathey through their involvement with the homeschool leadership of New Mexico. In getting to know them over the last few years, they and the other board members with CAPE (Christian Association of Parent Educators of New Mexico) have treated our family like we were honorary New Mexicans. Our kids and the Alberson kids are like cousins, and God has deepened our friendship with them in a special way these past two years, and especially so at the National Homeschool Leadership Conference in Colorado last year. Dennis and Cathey are really responsible for saving Chris's life at the conference and enabling him to be with us a few extra weeks. Cathey stepped in to help in countless ways while Chris was in the hospital and has become a dear friend for life.

Beth Raley

Beth and I have been very close friends for many years now, and she and her husband Ed have walked with our family through many of the ups and downs of Chris's MS as no other friends have. Beth has prayed for Chris and me in the wee hours of the night and all hours of the day. Beth flew out to Colorado with our son John last fall when he had to leave the set of the movie *Hero* to be with his hero, his dad, who had only a week or so to live. In Colorado Springs for the next ten days God used Beth as one of His instruments to help Chris prepare to make the transition toward leaving us and joining Christ in heaven.

Stan and LeAnn John

We met Stan four years ago when, in his capacity at Focus on the Family, he invited Chris and me, along with several other leaders to Colorado Springs to talk about homeschooling to FOTF staff. Chris and Stan kept in touch the next four

156

years and reconnected at last year's National Homeschool Leadership Conference. Little did we know then that Chris was going to make a rapid decline for the worse, and God would call him home just three weeks later. When the idea of hospice care came up as the best way for Chris to spend his last days on this earth, John and LeAnn stepped forward to offer their home to be Chris's last earthly home. They not only opened up their home to us, but their very hearts and lives as well. Stan and LeAnn enabled Chris's last days with us, his family, and with many friends and loved ones to be sweet and precious indeed.

Bob Farewell

I remember one of the first times Chris and Bob met at a homeschool convention in Massachusetts. Bob discovered Chris was an attorney for HSLDA and Chris found out that Bob was not only a homeschool dad, but a supplier of "living books" for homeschool families (homeschoolers love books!) and a Civil War reenactor. They were instant friends. Being fellow believers in Christ bound them together like blood brothers. Over the years our friendship with the Farewells has grown immeasurably; they are like family to us. In the last year of Chris's life, Bob was one of the few men who called Chris almost every week just to check in, pray with him, and share a few jokes and laughter. As the Proverbs say, Bob's merry heart did Chris a lot of good; it was like good medicine.

EPILOGUE

Bethany

On October 12, 2009, my father was finally healed from the multiple sclerosis that had been his burden to bear for fifteen long years. He went home to be with the One who was more precious than any other, and he left behind the eight people who love him the most. As his oldest daughter, my dad helped make me who I am today, and I will never forget the countless mornings we spent together going through *Beautiful Girlhood*, looking over my devotional notes from the previous week, reading the Bible while fishing in the canoe, and just spending one-on-one time alone with each other. Dad cultivated a relationship with each one of us kids and even though there are seven of us, somehow he managed to make all of us feel loved and important in our own special way.

Having spent the past six months editing and putting together this book, I was keenly aware of my dad's heart, his love for his family, his passion for sharing the gospel, and the incredible depth of his relationship with the Lord. My own heart broke when he died, but I can't help but be so very happy for him now because he is totally healed and in the presence of his beloved Savior. It makes it a little easier when I imagine what he's doing in heaven right now. I can just see him engaging in long conversations with Martin Luther and John Calvin, racing Eric Liddell, walking with the apostle Paul, and delighting in God's embrace.

I am so thankful to Shepherd Press and HSLDA, who helped get this book published, because I believe *Power Perfected in Weakness* has not only encouraged and blessed you the reader, but it has also been another opportunity to "hear" Chris Klicka one more time and get a glimpse of the man we will never see again here on this earth. This book, more than anything else he's ever written, gives you a glimpse into the heart and soul of my dad. You have seen his weaknesses, his struggles, and most of all, his triumphs through the help of his loving heavenly Father.

I miss him more than words can say. But I can see him running through the streets of heaven where he will never fall again. I can see him jumping and dancing with strong healthy legs that will never hurt or refuse to respond. I can see him singing in front of the throne of God with a strong and clear voice, both hands raised as he praises his Creator.

And, I can't wait to get there, too.

—*Bethany Klicka Arnoldbik*

Megan

My father was a true hero. He lived a difficult life. He fought battles for righteousness and justice's sake. He strove to be above reproach in all that he said and did. He loved good and hated evil, and he loved his country and more importantly, loved his countrymen. My dad cared for every soul on earth and wanted every man, woman, and child to know his Jesus. He shared the gospel with everyone he talked to and never failed to encourage those who were fellow believers in their walk with Christ.

Dad spent many hours praying for and with me. He stayed up late at night with me to listen to and counsel me. A day didn't pass that he didn't ask how I was doing and never once did he fail to thank me for any assistance I provided him with. Every night when I was done helping him, he prayed for God to bless me. Despite his obvious struggles and trials, he always cared about others. Daddy truly exemplified the fruits of the Spirit. He has left a wonderful legacy for my siblings and me to carry on, and a legacy that is passed on to every believer still here on earth to be faithful.

The last year had been hard for Daddy and I saw him yearning more and more for freedom from his earthly body and a wholehearted desire to be with Jesus in heaven. And he's home now. He is running and singing and rejoicing in the presence of his Savior. Dad was passionate about everything good on earth. He loved to taste, loved to see, loved to feel, loved to smell, and he loved the Truth. As I write this, I am listening to "You Wouldn't Cry" by Mandisa, a song sung by a loved one who has gone to be with the Lord.

When I heard that song for the first time, I broke into tears and I could see Dad dancing in heaven, joyously singing to me about his new home. Dad was passionate about everything here on earth even with all its imperfections; how much more excited he must be about true perfection. Dad's favorite song was "I Can Only Imagine" and Dad and I would listen to it and cry and just imagine that day and what it would be like to be with our Lord and Savior. I feel that "You Wouldn't Cry" would be Dad's new favorite song; his questions have answers and his dreams have become reality, and it's even better than he could ever have imagined!

I want to thank everyone who helped to make this book possible, namely my sister Bethany, who helped edit the entire text, and those at Shepherd Press who worked so hard to get *Power Perfected in Weakness* published. I am excited that everyone has the opportunity to read Daddy's last book. Through his final written work, Chris Klicka will continue to share the gospel despite his relocation to his new home.

May the Lord draw you nearer to himself as you read Chris Klicka's journey of faith and the story of Jesus' love and strength perfected in our weakness. *Thank you, Jesus, for giving me such a wonderful Daddy and friend who taught me about you. Please tell him I love him and can't wait to join him one day soon!*

—*Megan Hannah Klicka*

THE CLOSING

In the early stages of MS, even though Chris's health initially declined rapidly, we both convincingly felt an amazing sense of God's nearness. And it was God's nearness that would sustain us in the days, weeks, months and years ahead.

In 1995, after ten years of marriage and shortly after Chris was diagnosed with multiple sclerosis, we had six children ages seven and under. I was nursing twins, and we had four children in diapers. We were probably in the busiest season of our lives together. Our children tell me stories about those early days with our twins and I don't even remember them happening, so little sleep did we get back then!

When reminiscing about those days, however, I do remember so very clearly God's loving hand on our lives. In the midst of intense busyness and the unknown future of Chris's MS, He gave us the joy of our young children's voices in laughter and song around our home; He gave us joy in each other, in being committed as one mind and one soul to seeking after God with all our hearts. Most of all, He gave us joy in knowing Him. God's love for us and His sustaining power and hope made all the difference.

That is not to say we sailed on, carefree and happy-go-lucky through fifteen years of MS. The effects of the fall were deeply felt again and again in our marriage and in our family life. Communication was ever a challenge. Chris's desire to press on as though he didn't have a debilitating disease would test my faith in ways I had never experienced before.

For several years, while Chris was ministering to thousands of homeschoolers, who felt a connection with this humble servant and passionate advocate, though he deeply loved me, I felt like I was losing my best friend as the MS started affecting Chris's mind in ever so subtle ways. It made it more and more difficult for us to connect as we had always done. We both began to appreciate the glory of the cross of Christ for our sin more and more, and God used the suffering we endlessly faced to help us to lean harder on Jesus and depend less on ourselves.

Christ in Chris: The Hope of Glory

Over time, it was Chris's experience with MS that really made him a more loving husband, a better father, and a greater spokesperson for Christ. His testimony of being a sinner saved by grace, weak and needy, but having a faithful and mighty God struck a chord with many. I know our children have learned tremendously important life lessons by their father's example of daily dependence upon his Father.

Chris set forth a pattern for me of a dogged determination to be faithful to God—to continue to praise Him no matter what, to continue to serve Him no matter how difficult, to continue to obey His Word no matter the cost. He inspired me to press deeper into Christ, to find my Savior's strength in my weakness, and Christ's sufficiency for all my needs.

We were learning early on that only Christ could be everything we longed for, and so we mutually encouraged one another to find our all in Him. Chris knew he could not do the things he so longed to do for me—carry my suitcase or open a door. Gone were the days of taking walks on the beach, or dancing the old English country dances like we used to. "I still have you," I would reply. "That's all that matters."

Chris would often struggle with the reality of his slowly dying body—he lamented that he couldn't take the kids camping, throw a football around with John, or teach Jesse to shoot. He was so committed to our family; his heart was truly at home with us. I regularly tried to encourage Chris that he was able and was still doing the things that mattered most to the Lord. His love for us, his spiritual leadership—reading and teaching the Word to us, praying with and for us—and his humility and dependence on God were all things only *he* could do. Anyone could teach the boys how to play ball or shoot a gun. Only *he* could be his children's daddy. And God would encourage him once again in this truth, and give him joy for the journey ahead.

In his final year of life, Chris had a growing sense that God was preparing to bring him home to heaven. Following a hit-and-run car accident in December 2008, his MS symptoms progressed more rapidly and he developed an irreversible hypothermia that eventually led to his death in October of 2009.

Looking back over the last three weeks of his life, I am filled with a deep sense of gratitude for God's mercy. Chris was such a fighter, so determined to keep on keeping on, that had he been confined to a bed for months or years at the end of his life, he would have been plunged into despair. He was an amazing man—God gave him this supernatural grace to never give up, even though he felt like it countless times. Our family and friends can testify how he longed to go to heaven, to be set free from this earthly body and forever be in the presence of his great Savior!

At the same time, God's kindness was demonstrated in how He allowed Chris to live a full three weeks after going into ICU on September 25, and then nearly dying the next day from a urinary tract infection, pneumonia and complications from the hypothermia. Not only did the children and I get to spend much time with Chris, but many others, including Chris's and my parents, my brother, our pastor and several close friends both in Colorado and from all over the country. So in the best possible way, Chris's departure was short enough for him and long enough for us.

Our Last Good-Byes

In closing, I would like to share a story about Chris in his last hours of life on this earth with us. Two days before Chris passed away our oldest daughters Bethany and Megan flew out to Colorado to be with us for their dad's last days.

The next day, Sunday, Chris slept most of the day, so in the afternoon, our five daughters and I, at Megan's request, slipped away to the David's Bridal Shop for an hour or so. Megan had just gotten engaged three weeks earlier and for fun she wanted to look at wedding dresses with her five sisters and me.

With friends gladly staying at Chris's side while we took our little outing, the girls and I enjoyed the beauty of the sunshine reflecting off the fresh fallen snow on the way into town. When we arrived and started looking at racks of wedding dresses, I smiled at my girls and said, "How about this dress, Megan?" or "Oooh, look at this one!"

After several minutes, Megan held one up and asked, "What do you think of this one, Mom?" Taking one look at the dress I knew it was the perfect one for her, and replied, "Let's see if we can try it on, honey." The gentleman at the store had told us Megan couldn't try on any dresses without an appointment, but when we explained our situation to him, he capitulated with, "Okay, you can try on just this one dress."

When Megan put the dress on and stepped out we all couldn't help but respond with "oohs" and "aahs." Indeed, it was the perfect dress. Not only did it fit perfectly, but God blessed us with a special discount on the sale price. Little did we know that as Megan was preparing to be a bride for her bridegroom, Chris too, was preparing to meet his Bridegroom the very next day.

On Monday morning, Chris did not open his eyes once. I didn't know if he could hear my morning greeting or the words "I love you" that I had been saying several times a day for the past three weeks, or feel my arms around him in an embrace. I only kept doing what I had been doing every day since he went into the hospital.

As I sat there talking to him, I shared about our girls' outing the day before and how kind God was to let all of us be together when Megan found her perfect bridal gown. I told Chris I had so hoped he could see her in her dress before he went home, and as I was talking two little tears trickled down his cheeks.

He had heard! I know he would have loved to see his beautiful Megan in her wedding dress. I know, too, that Chris so wanted to be able to communicate his love for us at the end. It broke my heart to see his sadness. I imagined though too, that his tears were mingled with joy for Megan's future wedding, even as he understood he would be unable to be there. It meant the world to me just to know my dear husband would if only he could. His smile would have been the biggest of all.

An hour later, after the hospice nurse checked his vitals a second time, noting that Chris's blood pressure which had already dropped quite a bit from the night before, had lowered even more, encouraged me to get the children to come see and talk to their dad.

Immediately, I gathered them from around the house in just a couple of minutes. Moments later, when all seven of our children had gotten into the room, Bethany, our oldest daughter, said, "Hey, Dad, we're all here. We love you!" Chris took one more breath and then was gone. He ran straight into the arms of Jesus!

Where He Always Wanted to Be

I know to try to describe our sadness—the longing and aching in our hearts even still—would be impossible, so I won't try. I will share a picture the Lord gave me within minutes after Chris's departure.

I saw him with his old western boots and jeans on, running at top speed in heaven—boots and jeans just like he used to wear at Grove City College when he would run over to see me at my dorm—he was a senior and I was a freshman when we met. I pictured a huge smile (the one I love best) on his face and fellow saints yelling out greetings of welcome to him, some even asking him to stop and visit with them. And I heard his reply, "I've got to run for the Lord up here. I'm making up for lost time down on Earth. I'm praising God and have to use my legs to do it. Stop me in about 100 years, and we'll sit down and have a nice long visit!"

And two days before God brought Chris home, the Lord encouraged me to write this short verse:

No longer cloaked in frail humanity,
His spirit soars to gain Celestial joys,
Unimpeded by death's dark night
And free from the weight of sin's alloys.
My beloved sings! The object of his song
Is the One who bled and died for him,
No sweeter name did e'er he speak
Or treasure in his inner man.

I know with unshakeable certainty that the chaos of sin, suffering, trials, pain, loss and death DO NOT have the final say. Chaos must give way to God, who orders all things, who brings life out of death, healing out of sickness, rest out of chaos, and forgiveness for sin. For those in Christ, *rest and everlasting joy* are our reward!

—*Tracy Klicka*

O Lᴏʀᴅ, You are my God;
I will exalt You, I will give thanks to Your name;
For You have worked wonders,
Plans formed long ago, with perfect faithfulness.

For You have been a defense for the helpless,
A defense for the needy in his distress,
A refuge from the storm, a shade from the heat;
For the breath of the ruthless
Is like a rain storm against a wall.

The Lᴏʀᴅ of hosts will prepare a lavish banquet for all
peoples on this mountain;
A banquet of aged wine, choice pieces with marrow,
And refined, aged wine.

He will swallow up death for all time,
And the Lord God will wipe tears away from all
faces,
And He will remove the reproach of His people from
all the earth;
For the Lᴏʀᴅ has spoken.
And it will be said in that day,
"Behold, this is our God for whom we have waited
that He might save us
This is the Lᴏʀᴅ for whom we have waited;
Let us rejoice and be glad in His salvation."
—Isaiah 25:1, 4, 6, 8–9 ɴᴀsʙ

SPECIAL THANKS

Chris was a man who achieved great things for the glory of God, but he never could have done what he did without his family, friends and co-workers in the homeschool movement. I cannot presume to know all the people Chris would wish to thank were he here, but I would like to express deep gratitude and appreciation to the following people:

To our children Bethany, Megan, Jesse, Susanna, Charity, Amy and John—You are the main reason Dad did what he did. His love for you motivated him to be the great dad he was—leading you in God's Word, praying for you, listening to you and passionately desiring for each of you to know the same wholehearted love of and for your Savior he did. Thank you for being so faithful to your dad, for honoring him, loving him and serving him with your lives! May God answer every one of his prayers for you through the testimony of your faith as you walk in his footsteps.

To Mike Smith, president, HSLDA—Chris's love and appreciation for you was deep and personal. He regarded you as one of his very closest friends in the Lord. Not many people can say that of their boss. He was privileged to have one of the very best ones in the whole world. Thank you for the gift of your friendship.

To Mom and Dad Klicka—Thank you for being such supportive parents and so involved in Chris's life. Your prayers, encouragement and love through fifteen years of his MS meant so much to him. What an example of the love of Christ you have been!

To Chris's co-workers at HSLDA—Over the twenty-four years Chris worked at HSLDA, he regularly commented on how grateful he was to be working alongside you, serving the homeschool community together for the glory of God. He regularly said, "I *love* my job!" Thank you for helping to make it so easy for him to say that because of the love and camaraderie in Christ you all shared.

To the homeschool leadership community here in the U.S. and Canada—To Chris you were like family. You were the reason he worked so hard to get to his last National Homeschool Leadership Conference in Colorado Springs last fall, 2009. He knew it would be his last time with you, and because of his great love and appreciation for you, didn't want to miss it for anything in the world. Thank you for being dear friends and fellow co-laborers for homeschooling freedoms.

To the homeschool community in America—You are the ones Chris loved to serve through his work at HSLDA. So many of you were there to encourage and pray for him as he worked for the families in your state. One of his greatest desires at HSLDA was to encourage you as you raise your children for the Lord. If he could, I believe he would personally say to you, "Press on, friends, by the grace of God; your labors are not in vain."

To Joni Eareckson Tada, Dennis and Cathey Alberson, Beth Raley, Stan and LeAnn John, Bob Farewell and our friends at Shepherd Press—Thank you for your friendship to Chris and to our family, and for all you did to help make this book possible; great is my thanks to the Lord for each of you!

—Tracy Klicka

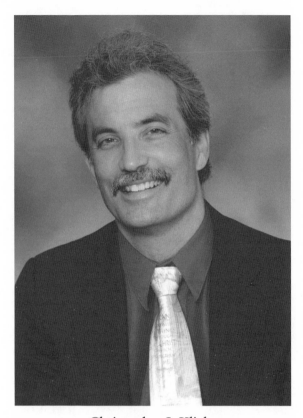

Christopher J. Klicka

Visit www.shepherdpress.com/ChrisKlicka

Tracy and Chris Klicka